No, For An Answer!

C.J RIGGS

Copyright © 2024 by C.J Riggs

All rights reserved.

No part of this book may be reproduced in any form or by any electronic or mechanical means, including information storage and retrieval systems, without written permission from the author, except for the use of brief quotations in a book review. Characters and events portrayed in this book are fictitious, any similarity to real persons, living or dead, is coincidental and not intended by the author.

Editing: C.J Riggs.
Cover Design: C.J Riggs.
ISBN:

DEDICATION

For all the women who are desperate for revenge,

but wouldn't last a day in prison…

Let Ashley be your guide.

PLAYLIST

Slow Down- Chase Atlantic

Fallout- Sleep Theory

Huggin & Kissin- Big Black Delta

Can You Feel My Heart- Bring Me The Horizon

Take Me First- Bad Omens

Sugar- Sleep Token

Daisy- Sorry X

Tipsy- J Kwon

Gun In My Hand- Dorothy

Lion Saint Mesa

Breaking The Habit- Broken View

You're Gonna Get What's Coming- Allergy & VG Lucas

Looking Glass- Slowave

Not All Men- Morgan St Jean

Rest In Peace- Dorothy

ACKNOWLEDGMENTS

First of all, I would like to thank my mum and my beautiful fiancé Lucy for constantly believing in me and always pushing me to be the very best version of my myself. I love you both to the moon and back. You each gave me the strength and courage to write my first short story and always made sure that I had the time to fulfil my dream.

I would also like to thank a small group of women that have hyped me up during the entire writing process and always made sure that my imposter syndrome was kept under wraps. My Cult of Lust, Autumn, Britt, Lisa, Megan, Unicorn (Sarah 1), Claudia, Aaliyah, Cyntia, Rose, Shae, Tess, and Sarah 2. All of the love and support you have given me, all the laughs and conversations we've had that would surely put us all in a mental institute, are memories I will always have close to my heart.

Jasmine Wallace, my sweet, sweet Jasmine. (Author of Demons Choice… Go buy that.) Thank you for spending countless hours reading my first draft and highlighting my terrible relationship with comma's lol! Thank you for always being available to answer any questions no matter how weird they were. You helped me understand grammar and punctuation in a quick video call, better than my primary school English teacher, lol. You are a diamond and a beautiful soul, and I love you.

Last, but not least… Ashley. The muse for *my* Ashley. Your crazy self, your desire to love and the support you give to others… is NOT the reason I chose you for my FMC. LOL… I chose you because you're just as sick and depraved as I am when it comes to extreme horror. However, your beautiful heart is the reason why I feel blessed to call you my friend. Thank you for always hyping me up and recommending me all the sick and twisted books you can. I love you.

Finally, my ARC readers… Just know I love each and every one of you. Thank you for all the time you spent reading Ashley's story.

Note From The Author

This is a dark, erotic horror novella, that includes dub/con, graphic depictions of murder, torture, and violence, as well as sexually explicit scenes, that are intended for an older audience. Below is a full list of triggers, and reader discretion is advised. If you find any of these topics distressing, please proceed with caution and maybe consider choosing a different book. This story popped into my head whilst shovelling cat shit from the litter tray, and I think that my brain might just be broken. Your mental health matters.

Trigger Warnings and Kinks Include:

Somnophilia, Necrophilia, Blood Play, Knife Play, Dub/Con, Graphic Violence, Sexual Assault, Rape, Death, Breath Play, Stalking, Fatphobia, Murder/Revenge, Suicide, Forced Orgasm, Grief and Loss Related To Suicide, Non/Con, Impact Play, Cum Play, Spitting, Choking, Anal, Maring and Biting, Degradation, Praise, Mental Illness, Mental Break, Institutionalization, Dismemberment, Castration, Blood, Gore, Decapitation, Revenge, Trauma, Torture, Vomit Kidnapping, Drugging, Skull Fucking, Paraphilia, Attempted Suicide, Hallucinations, Not HEA.

Again, I will repeat, your mental health matters! However, if you like the idea of a psychotic nineteen-year-old seeking revenge, then this book is definitely for you

THE SHADOW

Snap! Silence.

"Jesus fucking Christ." I lean back on my heels. Letting out a heavy sigh as I drop my head back and close my eyes. The sound of her neck snapping in my grasp, makes me feel complete. That took a lot longer than I initially anticipated. Mainly because I couldn't believe what I was witnessing. Stacy Cartwright was a fucking nutcase. The moment I mentioned for her to *'Run'* through the woods, the bitch got a smile on her face and excitedly took off.

These girls aren't like they used to be. The more dark romance that's getting flooded into the media is causing them to become fucking insane. It's a fucking pandemic. She ran for about five minutes and then said she "Got bored of waiting." She barely even put up a fight. She *accidentally* tripped three feet into the brush. It's like she wanted to die. Ok, nobody *wants* to die but come on.

That was just ridiculous. Nothing like my last kill. Nothing like Melanie. She was perfect and more than happy to suck my cock before I ended her life. So when I did eventually kill her, I had to take her throat with me and yes, I mean the entire thing. Oesophageal mass and all. They copped that one up to someone else because it didn't fit my usual MO. Which is a shame because I was really proud of her.

I mean, I'd only had my cock shoved down the back of her throat five minutes ago and with that little thing called 'Epithelials,' there was no way I could let that one slide. I just couldn't take a chance that some jobsworth cunt from the pathology department would have a penchant for thorough work and check every orifice twice.

I couldn't allow myself to be caught over something as basic as a blowjob. I'm not in any database but y'know, I was just being cautious. She's definitely in my top five for screamers too. Boy did she have a set of pipes on her.

At one point I thought I was about to jack off to her corpse, but no, I'm not *that* sick. That's for the psychos of the world. Anyway, back to Stacy. I've watched Stacy for weeks. Waiting for her to realise she was being watched. Waiting for that surge of panic to come from her, but there was nothing.

So I had to integrate myself into her life instead. Which I *really* hate doing. I had to go with the old *'I'm married so this needs to be kept a secret'* rouse. One thing I will say though, is I never fuck my victims before or after they're dead. It's just too risky. If I'm being totally open about it, I just don't like the idea of sex at all.

At one point, I thought there was something wrong with me, like I was broken or some shit, but my therapist told me I'm Asexual. That I only get sexually aroused when there is a connection. Which probably explains why I only get a massive hard on every single time I murder one of my girls. I dunno.

I'm a random person she met in a bar, and she just left with me. Like it was nothing. I even made an effort to be interested in her. No woman has ever kept me engaged in conversation enough to keep me in the room. I usually disassociate entirely, but I've mastered the art of making women think I'm interested. When I asked her if she wanted to try something fun in the woods she said yes before I even finished the question. Maybe Emo girls aren't my thing. Maybe I should stick to the innocent ones. Haven't had one of them in a long time.

I must put that on my to do list, so I don't forget. There wasn't even a flicker of apprehension when I pulled the mask and knife from my duffle bag. If I ever have children, I pray they're not as stupid as her. Because Jesus Christ.

As ridiculously unsatisfying as it was, at least she put up a little fight towards the end, when she realised I wasn't actually playing games. Usually, I stab the girls through the heart and make light work of removing it. Leaving it in a plastic Tupperware container by their head for someone to find.

I like to leave them visible in areas I know hikers frequent. That way at least their families aren't worried about them for too long. It's like *'oops daughters missing,'* nope just dead. Funeral. Grieving process. Done.

Yet, she was wriggling so much I didn't have time to grab my knife and I like to work while they're still alive. That way we both get to share the experience of their untimely death before the inevitably pass through blood loss.

"Fuck's sake." Looking back down at her lifeless body beneath me, her eyes still wide in fear. I lean forward and poke her tongue back into her mouth and shiver.

"Eurgh, nasty." Pressing her jaw up before rigor sets in. Nobody wants to die with their tongue poking out. This is usually the point where most people like me would fuck the corpse or rearrange it. I, however, don't have time.

She's also not worth the effort either. I'll just leave her here for the sweet old lady in the house to find. And by sweet, I mean cunt. This decrepit bitch cut me up on the freeway earlier in the day. So I followed her only to find out she lived in the middle of nowhere.

I'm straddling the limp body of Stacy in the old crone's back yard. I have to stifle a laugh because hopefully when she finds her, she'll have a heart attack and I'll kill two birds with one very small stone.

Usually that would fill me with some kind of rush, but tonight, nothing.

What gives?

Not even the vacant stare of Stacy's greying eyes is making my cock jump. Am I finally getting over this? Am I finally cured? The death rattle comes from her body and my cock jumps to attention.

"Oh thank god." I drop to all fours in front of her and suck in a deep breath. "Welp, I need to go home for a wank."

You can wank over me darling.

Hmm no Stacy I'm fine.

Is it something I did?

No, no it's not you it's me. I groan, dropping my head, careful not to touch hers because y'know, evidence. I might be brave enough to leave them in places that anyone could walk by and see but that's because I love the thrill of the moment.

Like when people fuck outside or cheat, the fear of getting caught sometimes outweighs the actual act itself. I snatch the necklace from her throat and jump to my feet. Pulling my sleeve back from my wrist I check the time.

"Shit!" I'm fucking late. I hate being late. I click my tongue and wink down at the body of the worst foreplay I've ever had and take off running.

Time to find the next one. Someone who's going to put up a fight this time.

ASHLEY

Why am I sitting here? Why on earth did I decide to park my fat ass on this stool? Inside this bar and allow *this* asshole to speak to me? His name is Clive. Yes, I know. Not exactly the sexiest name on the planet but I'm desperate.

I saw him on Link and decided that swiping right might be a good idea. Yet, as I sit here, I realise that his pictures really don't do him any justice, because he is actually quite handsome.

His personality, however, gives off 'Where's the clit?' Or 'Is it in yet?' I internally groan because this really isn't how I imagined spending my final night of freedom before I travel the final six miles with my mother to the town of 'Who gives a shit' to start my Sophomore year.

"Jamie?"

"Hmm?" I respond. I gave him a fake name. I'm here for something specific.

"I said your name like five times, babe."

Because it's not my name dickwad. And babe? So gross.

"Sorry. It's been a long day for me. A lot of traveling." I smile sweetly. It's surprising how lying has become such an easy thing for me now. Flowing out my mouth like air. Reaching over and brushing my fingers up his arm. I know this bible basher doesn't intend on fucking me.

It's all just a rouse. But preacher boy here looks like he's about to come in his pants any second. Plus, the hard on he's sporting in his khaki slacks proves to me that the gimp doesn't get touched by a woman very often. His priest… maybe.

"I think I should go."

You have got to be kidding me? That easy?

Please do because I am bored out of my ass. I've been sat here for over an hour now listening to him drone on about Jesus and how he saves and all that usual bullshit. I don't even think he's wet his wick yet. Twenty-five and already married to the church.

"Why don't you come by the church tomorrow before you leave."

Oh here we go again. The more I listen, the more I understand Judas.

He smiles as he puts the glass -that was once filled with a god damn cranberry juice- down on the table.

"Yeah, hard pass. I came here to get fucked tonight, Clive," I straighten myself. "Not to join a cult. So, thanks but no thanks." I shot the rest of my tequila and sit back in the chair. His jaw is hanging open now. I flick my hand in the air at him. "You're free to go God botherer."

"Jesus, Jamie."

"Eat my ass, Clive." I'm so bored of this right now. He steps back in shock.

"Sex out of wedlock is a sin." He points at me.

"And so are those fucking sandals you're wearing." He's looking at me now like I've grown a second head. Turning on his heel, he hurriedly walks out of the bar and into the night.

"I also don't think you're God would appreciate you being on Link either." I call after him. Laughing to myself as he practically runs the last few steps.

I stand up and make my way over to the bar to pay my tab. I'm praying myself that I won't make it that far. I didn't waste all my time here just to have this fail. I lean over the counter and signal for the bartender.

He raises a finger at me from the other end of the bar and smiles.

"Bad night?"

Bingo.

I turn to the left and lock eyes with the man beside me. His Emerald green eyes are framed with long dark lashes that women everywhere would kill for and a jawline that could cut glass. His thick, black hair is styled short around the back and sides, with a little length on top that sits perfectly pushed back from his face.

"You have no idea," I huff. The corner of his mouth twitches with a smirk as my eyes home in on his mouth. "You?"

"You could say that."

"Wife?"

"Single." He turns his body to face me slightly and it's then that I realise just how broad this man is. His muscular physique presses through the black shirt that clings to every curve of muscle on his arms and chest. Am I drooling? I feel like I'm drooling.

Focus Ashley.

"You?" He lifts his chin slightly.

"Very much so." I watch as his eyes flick to my lips then back up to meet my eyes and if I wasn't paying attention, I'd have missed the action entirely it was so quick.

"You plan on leaving?" He takes a sip of what I'm assuming is whisky. Leaning one elbow on the bar.

"Why you want to buy me a drink?" I chuckle.

"How old are you?" He lifts an eyebrow.

"Old enough," I shrug.

"You ready to pay darlin'?" the bartender asks from beside me. I don't, for a second break eye contact with him.

Buy me a drink.

"She'll have the same as what she's been drinking all night and I'll have a refill of Johnny blue please." He replies, not breaking eye contact for a single second. This man exudes confidence. He leans forward, pulling the seat out from the bar.

"Sit." He commands with a commandeering smirk, nodding his head towards the chair. I walk the short distance around the chair and hoist myself up. Crossing my bare legs between his widened ones.

"I'm Nathan."

I know.

I hold out my hand and he grasps it gently in his.

"Ashley," I breathe. My heart is beating ten to the dozen right now. Probably because I'm planning to fuck him soon. If things go my way. I'm not afraid of sex, in fact I love it. The way he's looking at me though, it's causing that organ under my rib cage to smash against my chest.

"I haven't seen you round here before." It's not a question. He sips the rest of his drink, just as the bartender replaces it with a fresh one, handing me a bourbon at the same time.

"Just passing through." My right leg that's crossed over my left is dangerously close to his calf. I very gently test the waters and -accidentally on purpose- slide my foot up the outside of his calf. The moment we connect, his eyes flicker with something that's similar to surprise. He's actually intoxicating, and I just want to lean in closer, take a deep breath and suck the smell right out of him.

If things were different.

"Thought I'd have some fun while I was here," I take a sip of my drink. "And seeing as I won't have to see anyone here ever again, I thought it was the perfect opportunity for it."

"You want to get out of here then?"

That was easy.

"Eager aren't you," I chuckle.

"A little."

"Hoping I'll say yes, or no?" I tilt my head.

He smiles broadly and leans in closer to me.

"I love a challenge. But we both know you're going to say yes. I've caught you looking over here a few times tonight." He looks me up and down. His lips barely touching mine but so close, all I'd have to do is lean forward and they would touch.

"The clocks behind you." I point.

He turns his head and laughs. "The clock. Right." Turning back to face me, he tucks a strand of my hair behind my ear, and I bit my lip. I knew I had him the moment I walked in here tonight. This was easier than I thought.

"If by eager you mean to bury myself so deep inside you that you scream. Then yes, Ashley, I'm very eager."

Fuck.
"Ok," I murmur.

The second we enter his hotel room; he pulls me back against the door. Caging me in with a hand on either side of my head. This motherfucker is tall but then again that's not very hard when I'm only five-foot-six and a size eight. His heavy breath fans across my face as he looks down at me, looking as though he's contemplating what he's about to do.

"Second guessing?" I ask.

"Just taking a second to look at you." The pad of his thumb presses to my bottom lip as he pulls it down. "Open your mouth." The words come so soft that my chest explodes with excitement. I know I'm here for a reason other than myself, but why not enjoy myself in the process. You know that feeling I mean. It's like when you wake up on Christmas morning, knowing Santa has been.

Or when you stole your first Chocolate from a convenience store. It's more than excitement. More than the usual butterflies in your stomach. It's fear and anxiety mixed with enthusiasm and desire. I must have been quiet for a beat longer than I thought because he leans in closer.

"Ashley, love, open your mouth for me." His voice now even lighter. I slowly open my mouth, looking up at him as he slides his attention to my widened mouth. Grasping the underside of my jaw he rests his thumb on my tongue.

A smirk playing at the corner of his mouth as he leans in further. I have to crane my neck to meet his eyeline and the burning sensation at the base of my skull is strong.

"Suck." I slowly close my mouth, wrapping my tongue around his thumb and gently sucking on it. A groan reverberates from his chest, sending goosebumps dancing all over my skin.

He has managed to incite a level of excitement in my body that I didn't think he could. I watch as his eyes flutter closed. There is nothing inherently sexual about sucking someone's thumb, but pair that with his British accent and my god, I'm a fucking puddle on the floor. I must've missed that from before. The loud music and chatter in the bar must've drowned his accent out slightly. I reach up, taking hold of his wrist and his eyes snap open.

"Take off my belt, love."

My nails slide down his shirt covered chest and I feel every single taut muscle that lies beneath it and my mouth waters with desire. Not breaking eye contact, I find the buckle and begin working it open, still sucking softly on his thumb.

Once the buckle is open, I stop. I want to go further, but for some reason, I think he will enjoy this more. A slow smile spreads across his face and he removes his thumb from my mouth.

"Good girl." Jesus Christ, he hasn't even touched me, his words alone are about to make me come.

"Tell me what you want, love." Taking hold of my throat and stroking it softly between both of his palms. I close my eyes and take a deep breath.

"I don't… I don't know." I do, but not yet. A deep chuckle fills the room. I can see why women have fallen for him.

"Yes, you do. I can see it written all over that beautiful face." His lips connect with my jawline, causing me to suck in a tight breath and another attack of goosebumps does the Mexican wave across my entire fucking body. My god he's fucking incredible. "Let me see those beautiful blue eyes, love." Another kiss. "Open your eyes baby."

Baby.

The word that would usually make me feel violently sick, could've possibly just given me what I love to call 'fanny flutters.' His voice is deep and guttural but posh at the same time. His words constantly enunciated when he speaks. I need to relax, or this will be over far quicker than I want it to be. But fuck me, he sounds like that fucking vampire from The Vampire Diaries all well-spoken and shit.

"I w-want to suck your cock." Why in the hell am I fucking stuttering? I know what I'm here for, but I've been in this room with him for maybe five minutes and already I'm a fucking mess. His eyes darken at my confession.

"Take it out."

Don't have to tell me fucking twice. My fingers scramble to the button on his black dress trousers and I make light work of the zip too as I yank it down and release his-

Fuck ME that's a big fucker!

His very thick, very big cock. Are all British men this big?

The palm of his hand rests on top of my head, gently pushing me to my knees and I willingly go. If this were anyone else, I'd punch them in the dick but seeing as Nathan here asked so nicely in that fucking disgustingly hot accent, I can't resist. I'd give him my entire bank balance if he asked for it.

Don't forget Ashley.

My knees hit the carpet of the seedy hotel with a thump and the simple act of me being on my knees makes alarm bells ring in my ears like shellshock. I'm on my knees for a strange man in a hotel room in the middle of nowhere and I'm so unbelievably turned on I can already feel my soaked thong against my shaved pussy. I don't know why I do it, but I look up at him.

"Good girl," he praises me, and I'm about to lose it. As a feminist, that 'good girl' shit is sickening. I'm not a fucking child, my guy. But again, hearing him say it just makes me desperately want to please him in any way he wants. He nods down at me, giving me the go ahead and I return my gaze back to the veiny, and very angry cock that makes my hand look childlike.

I poke out my tongue, flicking it across the head of his penis and licking the precum from his tip. The taste of him explodes onto my tongue and I groan. Hollowing out my cheeks I slowly suck him into my mouth at a torturous pace and work my hand up and down in a gentle twisting motion. I might have no gag reflex but there's no way this fucker is fitting all the way back there. But hey, I'll give anything a go.

"Fuck." He croaks from above me. Fisting his hand in my blonde waves. The tightening hold causing my eyes to water.

He pulls himself from my mouth and crouches down in front of me. "Open your fucking mouth wider, love. I'm going to fuck that throat till you choke." I immediately comply and open it as wide as I can. Why am I unable to dislocate my jaw like a snake and take all of him? Life just isn't fair sometimes.

Righting himself above me, he places one hand under my jaw and the other on top of my head and slides the tip of his cock in my mouth. I poke out my tongue and tip my head back slightly so I can accommodate him better.

"You've done this before. Such a good fucking girl," he croons and my inner goddess fucking screams at me.

This might be the sexiest fucking thing in my life and I'm just letting him treat me like this. He doesn't even give me a chance to fucking breathe before he thrusts forward. My eyes bulging out the sockets as the head of his cock hits the back of my throat and he holds it there.

"Fuuuck!" he growls. He drops his head back and even though my chest burns from the lack of oxygen I don't move. All I want to do is please him. Right here in this moment and I have no fucking idea why.

My chest constricts. My eyes begin to water and that all too familiar burn travels up my chest. The first choke releases and he pulls out immediately. Thick saliva connects from my mouth to his cock as he smiles down at me.

"Breathe through your nose," his tone confident and commanding.

"Fuck my face, Nathan. I can take it." He laughs then, so I slide my hands up the back of his thighs and pull him back to me. Back into the deep fuck hole that is my mouth and I suck him all the way to the base. He begins thrusting in me and my eyes roll back in my head.

The squelching sounds coming from his assault on my throat remind me of what it sounds like slushing through mud. The heavy grunts that come from his throat spur me on as he fucks my face. My drool dripping from the corner of my mouth as his thrusts get harder and he pulls out less and less. The tip of my nose is pressed against his pelvic bone as he takes a step forward, bending me back into a contorted position. I claw at his thighs for balance because, *what the fuck?*

"Get your hands off my thighs, love." Our eyes meet, tears spill over my cheeks. "Trust me," he commands. I nod as I let go of his thighs and allow him to suspend my weight back. "Now," he continues, "I'm going to come down that pretty throat and you're going to swallow all of it." The tone of his voice completely different from before.

"Nod if you understand." I nod once again. His other foot joins the other, one step behind my head and my knees burn from the stretch of my quad muscles.

He crouches down slightly, clasping the back of my head with both of his hands and thrusts into me over and over again as I cough and splutter. I count the eight thrusts before I feel his balls draw up against my chin and his warm, salty cum spurts down the back of my throat and I swallow. I swallow every fucking bit like it's the last supper and god himself blessed me with his Holy juice.

"Jesus, fucking, Christ!" The bark makes me flinch. Yanking himself free from my mouth I drop back onto my hands, my breathing frantic and irregular.

I sit there for a few seconds trying to catch my breath. Not for long though as he lunges forward, grabbing me under my armpits and hoists me up.

"I need to taste you. Put your legs over my shoulders and hold onto the doorframe." The way he just orders me about is making me fucking feral. Who have I turned into? Usually when I fuck someone from a bar it's over quicker than you can say 'thanks for the ride.'

Except here, with him, I don't want this to end. Hopefully, I get to fuck him more than once tonight. Hopefully, this is a man that will stay in my memory bank for a long, long time. One I compare all other sexual exploits with. He looks late twenties, maybe, but he fucks like he's older.

Right now who gives a fuck? Not me, because I wrap both my legs over his shoulders like he instructed. My back hits the door and I reach up, grasping the door frame like my fucking life depends on it.

"Come back to me, Ashley," his voice floating into my ears as I look down at him and watch as he slides his hands up the side of my thighs, ruching my mini skirt up to my waist. The action although nothing special, is unusually erotic to me right now. His hard, calloused hands grazing my soft, delicate skin deliciously slow.

"Watch me eat your cunt." Holy fuck, ok. I look down as he slides two fingers inside my neon green thong, running his nose up my slit and taking the deepest of breaths.

"Oh, fuck!" I cry out as he sucks my clit into his mouth at the same time as he thrusts two, thick fingers into my awaiting pussy. "Yes, yes, yes," I chant into the stuffy, sex filled room. I watch as he pulls his fingers from me and lifts me away from the door. I grasp the back of his head to balance myself before I'm thrown onto the bed with a thump. He drops to his knees in front of me, a devilish grin on his face as he pushes my legs wide and back against my chest.

"Hold them there and don't come." Lacing his fingers back into the fabric of my thong he pulls it over one ass cheek to give him a better view. I watch as he lifts me just under my ass and runs his flattened tongue over my back hole and up to my pussy.

"Holy shit!" I screech. The sounds of his enjoyment at eating both my ass and my pussy constrict my chest as they fill the room. I've never had someone eat my ass before and I must say, I'm not fucking mad at it. If the slurping and spaced-out moaning that's coming from his throat are anything to go by, then I think he's enjoying it just as much, if not more, than me right now.

"Oh shit. Please don't stop." I'm begging. Begging because he feels so fucking good. His rock-hard cock standing at attention as I look back down at the scene in front of me. If I'd have known this was going to happen, I'd have foregone my date with Clive, the sandal wearing, bible basher and made a move on Nathan the moment I walked into the bar. Because I knew he was there all along.

His broad, muscular back was the first thing I saw when I entered the dingy building and I also saw the side glance he gave me when I ordered my drink. I just got the feeling he wasn't interested by the way he broke the eye contact. I was clearly fucking wrong because the way he is devouring me right now is criminal.

"Fuck me… Please fucking fuck me!" I scream. He laughs. I groan. Lifting his hand, he smacks my pussy and I cry out again.

"Fucking beg for it, Ashley." He growls as he crawls between my legs.

"Please, Nathan."

"More."

"I need your cock inside me," I whimper.

"More, Ashley! Say what you really want. Don't fucking hold back."

If I die. I'm fine with it.

Dropping my head back against the mattress, I close my eyes tightly and fist the comforter. "Fill my cunt with your fat fucking cock!"

"That's my girl," he laughs at my announcement. My tone is laced with extreme frustration because I need him inside me. He reaches between us, lining himself up with my entrance and slides his cock up and down. Coating his length with my wetness. Then in one single, deep thrust, I've taken each inch of him inside me, and my mouth forms an 'O' as I scream out. Leaning up onto his forearms, he looks me dead in the eyes before he speaks.

"This won't be gentle, love. I needed to fuck you the moment you walked into that disgusting bar."

I crank my neck in his direction, running my tongue up and over his Adam's apple, all the way over his chin. I press my lips as close to his as I can without them touching and breathe. "Hurt me."

His eyes darken as he looks down into my eyes and I hope with every single inch of my being that he can see how desperately I want this. Need this. Need him even. Pulling back he slams his cock back inside me and a smile begins to form on both our faces as he fucks me hard and fast into a psychotic oblivion.

His thrusts are hard, the sound of his thighs slapping against mine as they connect. He's driving into me like I'm the last woman he will ever fuck and the feeling of him stretching me out is fucking painful at first. But the wetter I get, the more he talks dirty to me and the more I open up to him, the quicker the pain turns to fucking pleasure. Wrapping both hands round my throat, he squeezes and smiles down at me.

"Choke for me."

Black stars dance in my eyes before everything goes black.

ASHLEY

I drop the large cardboard box onto my bed. The last of my stuff from the delivery to my college dorm room. My mother was far too busy to help me move into the dorms as she was out with 'Skip.' That's not his name, I just call them that because they never stick around for too long and always end up skipping town on her.

Not that there's anything wrong with my mother, she's stunning. She's just a glutton for punishment when it comes to men that are no good for her. But this time it worked out in my favour.

It's one of the reasons why we moved up here in the first place. I was lucky enough to get a spot at Brown halfway through sophomore year, thanks to the man my mother is currently dating. I tip the delivery guy who helped me bring everything up and I watch as he looks down the front of my black vest.

"Aint nothing in there for you."

The smug bastard simply smiles at me like he has the right to. I usher him out of the room just as another girl -who I'm assuming is my roommate- barrels in almost knocking me on my ass. Grabbing my shoulders she steadies me, giving the delivery guy a stink ass look.

"Shit. I'm so sorry."

"It's fine." It's really not.

Fit in Ashley. Remember.

Make sure everything goes to plan while you're here.

"I'm Mia. You must be Ashley, right?" A wide grin stretches across her face. Great, she's one of those happy ones. Why couldn't I just be paired with the goth kid down the hall. I need to make this work, I need to at least try and fit in while I'm here. For the small amount of time, I plan to be here anyway. Then I can go back to being my miserable self. Like I've been for the last twelve months.

"On all accounts." I mirror her smile, holding out my hand and trying to act as normal as possible. I look nothing like I used to a few weeks ago. Everything about me is different now and after everything, this is how I'm going to fit in.

"Ew, no." She smacks my hand out the way and pulls me in for a tight hug. Yeah, this one's bubbly. "We hug here." Pulling back from the overly tight embrace she looks at the boxes strewn across the room and grimaces.

"I'm sorry," I wince, tucking a strand of my wavy, shoulder length hair behind my ear as I bend down to pick up a box. "I'll make sure this is all done before the end of the day."

"Girl, it's fine." She waves her hand in front of her face. Dismissing my worry and I instantly relax. She doesn't seem so bad so this could work. "You want some help?"

"Uh, sure."

The both of us work in silence to start off with. I separate the boxes she can help me unpack from the ones she doesn't really need to touch.

Like my underwear or personal items. It takes us pretty much all day and considering classes don't start for me until Monday. I'm free to look around campus and town for a bit. Get my bearings on where everything is so I can make sure I'm not late to any of my classes. I didn't expect to be finishing my sophomore year here ether but luckily my grades were good enough to transfer me too and they surprisingly had an opening.

"So, tell me, Ashley," Mia begins. "Where you from?"

"Ohio originally. You?" I rip open the box beside her.

"Right here in town." She laughs, opening up my box filled with trainers and placing them neatly in what seems to be my side of the wardrobe. "What brought you here in the middle of your first sophomore year?"

"My mother," I chuckle. This acting normal bullshit doesn't come easy, and I give myself the ick just trying to come across like that all-American, cute valley girl. "She got into a new relationship. This time, I was lucky enough to benefit from it. The guy she's dating got me in as he's a big donator to the school or some shit." I shrug, placing my underwear in one of the three drawers in the dresser that's available to me. "My mom loves men."

"Yeah, my dad has that problem. Except he does it while still being married to my mom."

"Jesus," I frown.

"Nope. Just an asshole," she chuckles dryly from beside me. We continue to put everything away and spend most of the time talking and getting to know one another. She's not bad for a roommate. At least being in this dorm situation will be a little easier.

Mia doesn't seem like the nosey type which makes things a lot better for me. The less she asks, the less I have to lie about why I'm here in the first place.

I was supposed to be here with my best friend Maisy. I always promised we would share a room together when we got accepted into university. When she got accepted into Brown and I to Penn State, we practically lost our minds. But here I am now. Even if it is a little late.

"Oh, cute." Mia sings from beside me. I turn from where I'm bent over a box and see her holding a photo frame in her hand. *The* photo frame. "This you?"

She smiles broadly as she looks over the image in the black frame. Standing up, I walk to her, taking it out of her and looking down at it. Nobody would be able to tell this is Maisy considering we're both eight here.

"Yeah, me and my best friend." I smile. Both of us with an arm around each other's shoulders, an ice cream in the other.

"So adorable. You guys close?" She asks as she continues hanging my clothes in the wardrobe.

"We were."

"Oh, what happened?" All the air is immediately sucked out of the room. The moment the words sail from my lips and into the atmosphere, it turns thick with awkwardness. My chest and throat strained.

"Just different paths in life. I haven't seen her for about a year now."

Evidently true.

"That sucks."

"It's fine." I cut her off, smiling as I place the frame on the table beside my bed. Facing me as usual so I wake up to her beautiful face like always. Maisy was my whole world and I'm pretty sure I was hers at one point too.

Then everything went to shit, and now our friendship is broken.

"What happened? If it's ok for me to ask. If not, I'll shut my mouth."

"She uh," there's no need for me to go in depth about our relationship. She doesn't need to know, and, in all honesty, I don't really need to tell it. "She just gave up. On us. On our friendship." I take a deep breath and continue unpacking some things from the box in front of me. "I guess things just got too much y'know?"

"I get it." She shrugs, completely oblivious.

Which is exactly how I need it.

"How about we go get a fucking drink."

I laugh then. "Mia, it's three in the afternoon."

"Five somewhere, right?" Wiggling her shoulders playfully she sticks out her tongue and all I can do is roll my eyes.

"Fine. Where to?"

"OBK." She winks.

"OBK?" I question. "Is that some kind of bar?"

"It's a frat house just off campus."

Shaking my head softly I decline. "Mia, I'm sorry I'm just really not in the mood for all this. I just spent like two days driving."

Lie.

"All I want to do is rest. I have a lot to catch up on."

Also, lies.

I have nothing to catch up on. I've spent the last three months catching up on the syllabus and taking online classes to make sure I could keep up with all the other students. Not that I really need to. I have a 4.0 GPA.

I just wanted to make sure there was nothing to fuck up my time here. Although it will be a short period of time.

"I'm already half way through the semester and-"

"I hate to break it you Ashley, but, as my roommate, it's a standard requirement. I'm sure if you and Maisy were still friends, she would want you to enjoy yourself?"

No.

Maisy would've wanted me with her.

But she left before we had the chance to talk.

"Mia, I don't know."

"Look," she removes the stuff in my hands and places it on the bedside table. "How about we go get some Pizza instead, come back here and watch a few movies?"

"That sounds a lot better."

The weekend came and went. I spent most of that in the presence of Mia and the cheer team that she just got accepted for a spot with. Who'd have thought I'd be here, forcing myself to play the part of a highly excitable teenage girl.

I didn't want to be out and about with the cheer squad, in fact I hated listening to them drone on about their bullshit problems. Like their lives are much worse than other people. Most of the time all they need to worry about is what shade of lip gloss they're going to wear. They all come from rich families and don't know what it's like to struggle. Fucking stupid. The only person I've really gelled with is Mia the past few days since I started here.

In school I was never the popular one. I was the one who was profusely teased about the way I looked all through kindergarten, until the day I met Maisy. We became best friends. Maisy was the complete opposite of me in every single way.

She was brunette with honey-coloured eyes and had the most beautifully pale skin. Her naturally pink lips, and heart shaped face were beautiful. She always looked like she was wearing makeup. A natural beauty everyone would say. Then there was me.

Chubby Ashley. The one that no one looked twice at, the one who nobody paid attention to. She always had a way with the boys in our high school and always made sure everyone either hated her or wanted to be her.

Everyone except me. I loved her though, more than anything, but I didn't want her life. I was happy being me. Boring old Ashley. Everything changed over the summer I turned seventeen. I came back from science camp a little slimmer, a little blonder and a lot more tanned.

My breasts grew an enormous amount and Maisy hardly recognised me. After that, I started to get noticed more. It was the final year of high school and soon enough I started to become a little more popular. Shortly after Maisy's sophomore year, she changed. She became someone I didn't recognise, and I tried desperately to get through to her and find out what was wrong. But she refused to tell me. Refused to even talk to me.

After a while I barely had any contact with Maisy at all. It's like I didn't exist anymore. Like our friendship meant nothing to her. I called numerous times a day and, in the end, our friendship died. Then, last year I learnt something that I'll never forget until the day I leave this earth.

It's what brought me here. Why I convinced my mother to uproot our life and come here for the man she loves and the new job she wanted. All that made it easier and considering he is a big donator to the science department; I got in nice and easy.

Because I needed to be here. Pushing the thoughts of Maisy and the incident from my mind I knock on the large wooden door in front of me and patiently wait for it to open. The door swings open and I'm greeted with the fattest fuck I think I've ever laid my eyes on.

Christ almighty.

Joseph Chambers stands in front of me in all of his rotund glory. I've seen pictures of the guy from twenty years ago and I'm being honest, he was a total fox. Think Biden in his teens.

Although the man that's greeting me now is a shadow of his former self. He's wearing a checkered suit with a fucking pocket watch hanging from the waistcoat that was far, far too small for him.

"Ashley Porter?" He questions, raking his eyes over my entire body and the shiver that runs up my spine makes me sick. He takes no shame in lingering on my breasts. Taking in a deep breath as he focusses there for longer than is legally necessary. The guys like fifty.

Gross.

"That's me," I grin. Trying my best to give him the most convincing smile. When really all I want to do is stab him in the eye with the biro I have in my purse.

Sick fuck.

"Please," He motions his arm to the side. "Come in and take a seat at my desk." I walk in and I swear he breathes me in as I walk past.

Typical creep.

I drop my bag beside me and take a seat. It's not like I'm wearing anything remotely slutty today either. The outfit I decided on today is a lot tamer than most girls around here wear. While I'm here I need to stand out but in a very subtle way. I'm wearing dark blue jeans and a black t-shirt. Paired with my favourite black and white Chuck Taylors. Nothing crazy. Nothing that would make a man desperately look over me like I was the first woman he's seen in over a thousand years.

"So, tell me Ashley, how was the drive down here?" Walking round the table he squeezes his lardy ass into the swivel chair behind his desk and I do everything I can to supress the grimace on my face. Jesus this guy's fat. The way he's looking at me too, is just the same as every other man who wishes they could have me but can't.

"It was fine, thank you. My mother starts her new job next week so she's just relaxing while I get myself ready. Thank you again for accepting me on such short notice. I know my step father really appreciates the kind gesture." He waves his hand in front of me, rejecting the comment entirely.

"It was no problem at all. We had a vacancy last minute and what with your step father being a very good friend of mine, as well as a very big contributor to Brown, it would be rude of me to turn him down." Again, his eyes rake over my body, focussing on my swollen breasts that are propped up in my lace bra. His tongue darts out and wets his bottom lip. God men are sickening.

"Well, I appreciate it all the same," I smile again. "I worked so hard during the summer. Enough to get my brain, mind, and body into shape for the coming year."

"I hear you were a gymnast at your previous school." It's a rhetorical question, one I don't need to sit there and answer, but the way his eyes continue to settle on every single part of my body, it makes me feel vile. Still, I work the hardest I can to try and make sure I give the most confident smile I can muster.

The muscles in my face are strained within an inch of their life as I continue to smile. Do people smile this much in general or am I trying too hard. I wouldn't even know how to act fucking cheery if my life depended on it. I've masked my entire life, but no more than I am right now. Masking has always come easy to me.

Few people would understand what it's like to have to hide who you really are on a regular basis, and how hard and time consuming it can be to act like someone you're not. I'm happier than anyone would be in this moment. I'm right where I need to be, and nothing feels better.

"I can't wait to start assisting the professor of the Criminal Psychology department." I sit back in the seat a little more. And he follows me incredulously. This man really has no shame whatsoever. It's like he doesn't care at all if a young girl catches him staring. I feel uncomfortable and if I could, I'd end this conversation right here and right now. I can't though, this man here is the sole reason I've even had a chance to become a TA.

I put in so much hard work for this spot, managing to push all other contenders away. He was very dubious at first, as most girls that apply are usually doing so to try and get into the professor's slacks, I guess. Once I fed him the lie that I was already in a relationship back home, his dismissal of me during that interview became far lighter than I expected.

"I'll tell you what sweetheart, how about I take you to meet Professor Danvers. You'll be assisting him this year."

"Sounds good." I widen my smile and stand with him as we make our way out of the office and down the hall.

Nathan

"So, now that we've navigated through the difference between a Sociopath and a Psychopath, can anyone tell me what three things differentiate the two?" I lean back on my desk, looking up at the students in the curved seating area and wait for one of them to speak. "Anyone?" It's the beginning of sophomore year and I've yet to find a single student that stands out in my class. "Yes?" I point to the student who has raised their hand.

"Is this going to be on the exam?"

Fuck me dead.

"Yes Julia, this is definitely going to be on the exam." Jesus. Fucking. Christ. I look around the room and sigh. "Why don't you all just gather your things and go. I want three chapters read of your Criminal Profiling textbook and we'll go through it next week." The students begin to scramble for their things, desperate to remove themselves from the class. My last sophomore class was phenomenal and it's like now I'm stuck teaching the town of deliverance about how to make fire.

Walking around my desk, I begin to gather my own things. Waiting for a few moments until the room becomes deathly silent. Removing the glasses from my face, I rub my eyes and pinch the bridge of my nose. This is fucking horseshit I didn't come here to teach fucking idiots.

"Nathan."

I look up to see Joseph Chambers -Dean of the University admissions- walk his fat, swollen body through the side entrance to the classroom that's situated next to my desk. Joseph Chambers was one of the few people at this place that I actually tolerated. The man looks like an overstuffed chipmunk at the taxidermy office in town and honestly, I'm surprised his wife has stayed with him for as long as she has.

The clothes he's wearing are clearly a size smaller than necessary. He knows this but does absolutely nothing to change that. Not like me. Not at *all* like me. Most of the time I keep myself to myself. I come here, go to the gym, go home. Eat, sleep, repeat. This is a place of work, not a social club. I didn't get to where I am today without sacrificing certain things in my life so I could be the best at what I do, and I am the best.

I was head hunted for this place because I was the best, I excelled in all aspects of excellence and with everything I had to offer, there was no way they weren't going to give me everything I asked for. After all I was packing up and moving half way across the fucking globe just to work here.

I've won many prestigious awards in my time and now, finally being here at Brown, it gives me a chance to expand myself and my knowledge. To push myself for further achievements.

I've been here now for three years, and I've worked my ass off sucking up to the man standing in front of me. Just so when the time comes to him deciding who will take over as 'Dean of Admissions', I'll be at the forefront of the old bastard's head.

"Joseph," I smile, taking his hand in mine and giving it a brief, yet solid handshake. "What can I do for you?"

"I have you're new TA waiting outside the classroom. Would you happen to have five minutes spare, so I can introduce the both of you. She's a transfer student from Penn state. 4.0 GPA and very eager to learn all she can. Sweet kid too. Nineteen I think."

Nineteen. A bit younger than I was hoping for but beggars can't be choosers.

"Of course, bring her in." A 4.0 GPA? Transferred? For what, I wonder. I look up as the door clicks against the framework and the moment I do; all moisture leaves my mouth. My heart begins to hammer so heavily in my chest I feel as though it might burst through the bony cage its encased in.

"Nathan, this is-"

"Ashley." I murmur. All sense instantly leaves my brain the moment I lay eyes on the girl before me.

Shit, shit, shit. SHIT!

This can't be happening to me right now. Jeeesus. Fucking nineteen. She was nineteen when I… Fuck! Rape. Wait, statutory rape is anyone under sixteen in the US, so I'm clear of that.

Ok, good. But fuck me I'm thirty-eight and she's… she's… She's nine-fucking-teen. Almost twenty years my junior. Not that I look my age. I look exceptional for my age really, and *she* didn't look her age either.

Not the least bit nineteen when I had her on all fours, taking my cock so far down the back of her throat it was criminal, all the while I was leant forward, and finger fucked her-

GET A GRIP DANVERS!

This is not the time to think about shit like that. Hold on, my job? Is my job safe? I mean technically speaking she hadn't even started yet. But she was enrolled.

Shit!

Although it *was* before she came here. I can't really get into trouble if they found out. I'd just be known as the nonce who liked to fuck little girls.

The things I did to her.

She was in a bar. I just assumed she was twenty-one.

If they do find out about it, it will also affect my position as Dean next year. God almighty, this cannot be happening to me. I'm a fucking paedophile.

"Nathan?" Joseph waves his hand in front of my face. Bringing me out of my dissociative stupor.

"Sorry, Joe, I spaced there for a second. Realised I forgot to tell the students what chapter to read for next week's class." Lies, all lies. I'm shitting a brick.

"Always works hard this one." He claps a hand on my shoulder and grins. Turning to face the angel I fucked three ways from Sunday a few days ago with a broad smile. "Ready to insert himself anywhere."

Kill me now.

"Oh, I'm sure he is," Ashley giggles. Covering her perfect little mouth that was made for sucking cock, and here I am, again, thinking about her like that. I need to stop, this is so fucking inappropriate of me.

Granted, sex with Ashley was quite possibly the best sex I've ever had in my entire god damned life and that says a lot. Connection is a massive thing for me, and I never just go out and fuck random strangers.

For some reason though, that night at the bar I just couldn't resist her. She was fucking perfect.
Nonce mate.
Ashley holds out her hand to me and leans in. Her picture-perfect, small-town girl image causing me to go rigid. "It's really nice to see you again, professor."
"You've met?" Joe questions, his brow creasing in confusion as he turns to face me.
"In the hallway earlier," Ashley interrupts, dropping her hand from mine and covering for me. If I had to speak right now, I'd stutter like a little bitch. "I was trying to find English Lit," she continues. "Right?" Meeting my eyeline for the second time. Fuck, I dazed off again.
Shit, shit, shit.
I'm going to jail. Jesus H. Christ.
Nineteen?
"Yes," I clear my throat. "Poor girl was wandering around the hallway like a lost puppy," I chuckle. Can he smell the child predator on me?
"Well, it's rather big that's for sure." He laughs this time. "Anyway," he shoves his hands into his checkered slacks.
His rotund belly hanging over it like a fucking apron and I have to stop myself from gagging. "Ashley here will be starting with you as of tomorrow. I have to leave but talk between yourselves and set up details of timings and everything so she's here to best support you."
He nods and turns on his heel to leave. The door clicks closed, but I can't take my eyes off of her. I need to sit down. Pulling my chair back, I drop down and sigh. Resting my elbow on the arm of the

wooden swivel chair, I throw my fist to my mouth. Taking a small step forward she presses her hand to the oak table, leaning forward slightly to meet my eyeline. The action so smooth that I almost find myself shuddering as I watch her. Willing for my cock to stay asleep.

"Nathan I-" I hold my hand up, cutting her off.

"Nineteen? Did you plan this?"

"What?" She frowns, hurt lacing her eyes. "No not at all. How was I to know you were the teacher of the class I'm not only taking but assisting too?" I search her eyes for any inclination that she might be lying. I've been teaching criminal psychology for thirteen years now and I know all the facial expressions of a manipulator. Yet here, on her, I'm coming up empty. There's not a single micro-expression on her face and I don't know if that makes me feel better or worse.

"You understand that what happened between us can never happen again, right?"

She steps around the desk and sits on the corner. The book that her hand is wrapped around, placed gently in her lap as she looks down at me.

I grip the opposite arm of the chair until my knuckles go white and I lose all feeling in my fingertips.

"I really didn't know, I swear."

Her breasts jiggling slightly as she speaks. Oh my god. Stop. "Ok. But this is now strictly a student-teacher relationship." I stand from the chair.

Towering above her and as the air swirls around me, the scent of her fruity perfume sails into my nose and I have to suppress a groan. Locking it away deep in my chest.

"Of course," she agrees immediately. Nodding her head as she says the words.

"Meaning, nothing but work-related conversations. No flirting. No," I swallow as I remember what it felt like to have my cock buried inside her, "touching of any kind." She giggles then and the sweet sound flicks my memory back to three days ago when I called her a *'dirty fucking slut'* and she found it hilarious.

"No touching and no flirting... Got it," she nods. "Friends?" She smiles, holding out her hand to me again. She slides her hand in mine ever so softly and grips it as hard as she can. "Ashley Porter. TA, Gemini, and I love Chinese food."

"Nathan Danvers," I counter, trying my best not to smile. "Scorpio but Thai is better." I drop her hand and she places it back in her lap.

"I also have a penchant for older men too it seems," she winks at me, standing up and flicking her long, curly blonde hair over her shoulder.

"Ashley," I sigh.

"Too soon?" she smirks.

I blow out a frustrated breath and begin packing my things up again. "I'll need you in class tomorrow at eight AM, no later. Please read chapters one through seven of-"

"The Psychology of Criminal Conduct by James Bonta and D. A. Andrews as well as the Psychology of Crime by Philip Feldman. Done."

I snap my head to her, and she grins. "Done?" I query. Surely not.

"Yeah, done. I've read them both twice. Both extremely contradictory in their own right. However,

I did enjoy Feldman's analysis on criminal behaviour based on the biological aspect better."

If I didn't want to fuck her before, I definitely want to now.

"Impressive," I nod.

"Go hard or go home, right?" her shoulder lifting in a delicate shrug.

"You'll be prepared for tomorrows lecture then." It's not a question. Pulling my tan, leather satchel from the desk, I hold out my palm, indicating for her to walk first. Turning on her heel, her hair flicks over her shoulder and I'm greeted with that fucking coconut shampoo that I haven't been able to stop thinking about. She's absolutely perfect in every way but it can never happen again. I have to keep repeating that as I follow her out the door, eyes strained to that perfectly round ass of hers. Locking the door to my classroom, I turn to face her. "I'll see you tomorrow Miss Porter-"

"Eight AM bright and early." She winks as she walks backwards. Swinging back around after a few steps and disappearing around the corner.

I'm completely fucked.

ASHLEY

I look up as the door to the classroom opens and Professor Danvers walks in. A coffee in one hand and his leather bag in the other. It's been a week since I started working as his TA and kudos to him, Nathan has stuck to his previous statement of us never happening again. He hasn't looked at me or touched me inappropriately at all. Much to my dismay and utter frustration.

I've tried everything I can over the past week to get him to crack. We have spent a lot of time together. Grading papers to which I've always made sure to sit as close to him as possible. Grazing his hand, leaning over the table to grab a highlighter I really had no necessity for. I've even worn clothes that were the tightest fit I could muster.

I've made sexual innuendos, flirted, bent over his desk so my ass was high on show and the man still refuses to crack. Jesus, I've made sure my fucking tits were on show at one point, and nothing. But I still have time. I'm not one for giving up. When I want something, I always get it and I don't just want this man, I need him. I know what he's capable of and I'm willing to bet that a little push over the edge will clear things up.

Most of the time, if Mia is at cheer practice or in class and when I have a free period, I find myself laying on my bed, finger fucking myself while thinking about all of the nasty little things I'm going to do to him when I get the chance. Last week I fucked myself vigorously with the eight-inch dildo I have under my bed. Fucked myself raw and it still wasn't enough.

Nothing has been able to stop the burning need to have him stuffed inside of me again because the more he fucks me, the more he will want me and the more addicted he becomes, the more I have *him* right where I want him. I need to focus though, and not let things distract me from my end goal. I'm on a hiatus right now and soon enough, I'll eventually get what I came here for.

I always do. He's not the first man, and he definitely won't be the last. Complete the task at hand and be free to move on and continue with the next one on my bucket list.

I've been here since Seven AM.

The janitor Steve didn't take much convincing after I begged him to let me in early so I could get some of my paperwork done and prep for the class. Nathan, sorry, Professor Danvers emailed me over a list last night of things that I needed to get complete for him. Ready for his morning lesson. He explained in the thread, I would only need to complete the top three and the rest he would take care of.

However, I had a feeling that after finding out the particulars of my age, and pretty much having a stroke on the spot, he might not have the brain power to complete them. So, considering I barely sleep, I did.

"Miss Porter. You're early," he states. God this Miss Porter shit really is annoying. I plaster a smile on my face and stand, gathering the paperwork and meet him at his desk as he places his coffee in the middle.

"Couldn't sleep." I respond.

Because I couldn't stop thinking about your cock.
And my plans.
And everything else.

"Am I working you too hard?" he asks, and as I smirk, he realises his mistake.

"Not hard enough," I mumble, looking back down to my laptop.

"What was that?" he chuckles.

"I said… You're not working me nearly as hard as I want." I watch as the thoughts running through his mind contradict themselves over and over again as he stares into my eyes. Debating whether he should continue this barrage of sexual insinuations. I stand up from the small table in front of him and pace over.

"I did everything you asked of me on the email-"

"Shit!" he exclaims, dropping his satchel on the table and pinching the bridge of his nose.

"What?"

"I left the fucking Pop Quiz on the kitchen counter."

"Oh, that's fine I-"

"It's not fine Ashley!" he snaps. I instantly close my mouth. "Nothing about this is fine! I worked all night on it and because of-" He meets my eyeline, his green eyes boring into mine as though he can see right through me.

I don't like it.

"I'm sorry," he sighs. "I shouldn't have shouted at you it's just-"

"It's fine. You seem pretty stressed." I round the desk and stand beside him. A little closer than necessary but I can't help it. My shoulder grazes his chest briefly and I feel him instantly stiffen beside me. "Is there anything I can do to help?" I turn to look at him. I want him to trust me. No, I need him to trust me.

Fuck, he smells incredible.

"No, I… uh, I'm fine." He clears his throat, rubbing the back of his neck. A tight smile on his face. It's never been this hard for me to crack men before. Nathan, however, is a tough nut to crack and I know why.

The fucker is nervous. I bend forward, placing the pile of papers on his desk and start sifting through them.

"I took the liberty of completing everything on the list. Y'know to, uh, make today easier. Just in case." I turn my face to him as he watches me in silence. His hand pressed to the table, a hairs width away from mine. I shouldn't want him; I have a plan and I need to stick to it. That's when I feel it. His thumb slowly grazing across my pinky finger.

"You did all this last night?" It's like he can't quite believe I managed to do it.

"As I said, I haven't, uh… I haven't been able to sleep."

"I'm sorry. I didn't mean to shout," he whispers. The tone of his voice making my chest pound. His warm breath coating my skin so sinfully. I suck in a breath as he curls his hand around my wrist, gently tugging me to him and my shoulder hits the centre of his chest.

You have GOT to be kidding me.
This is all it took.
Doing some extra fucking paperwork for the asshole.

"Why haven't you been sleeping?" Demanding I answer him.

"I uh," I look up at him through my long lashes.

"Use your words, love," he breathes the last word. So softly I could barely hear it, but I know it was there. "Tell me the truth as to why you haven't slept."

Squeezing my eyes shut, I answer. "I haven't been able to stop thinking about you," I respond, with a hint of sweetness as I bite my lip.

"Hmm." The small acknowledgement burns into me, and I can't bring myself to look up at him. Turning my palm, he presses my hand to his rock-hard erection. Just as big as I remember. I fake a shudder the moment his lips connect with my ear as he inhales deeply, his nose pressed to my hair. "Would it be inappropriate of me to tell you how I haven't been able to stop thinking about you either?"

"Very," I breathe, my eyes fluttering shut. I need this. I've finally got him. His words screaming out in my brain. I turn my head towards him. It's seven-thirty and soon the rest of the student body will be cramming through the university doors like rats. So right now, I have to do everything I can to make sure this is over with as quick as possible. Mainly because my goal doesn't involve half the student body walking in on us like this. It needs to start as a secret and stay that way.

"I've been trying my fucking hardest to stop jumping over my desk every fucking lesson and fucking you raw in front of the other students."

There we go.

"Pushing you to your knees and choking you with my cock. Last night, I fucked my fist to the memory of you on your knees begging me for it." My eyes shoot open, and I look into his. Yet where his eyes were once an emerald, green, they're now pitch black. I shudder. The excitement for what's to come, crawling up my spine.

"Tell me what you want to do to me Nathan." I look at him dead in the eyes. Challenging him. Mainly to see if he's all talk now or if this is going to be the start of everything I need.

"I'm going to fuck you, Ashley, over this desk. Do you understand?" He takes hold of my jaw in his warm hand, squeezing slightly. Heat blooms beneath my skin at his admittance, and the tiny hairs on my arms stand at attention.

"But it's seven-thirty. The class will be full soon." I act so well I almost convince myself.

"Stay right where you are," he winks. Stepping behind me and pressing his palm to my lower back. "Place both palms on the table for me, love. Spread the papers out in case anyone walks past the side door, that way it will look like you're reading through work for me."

I do exactly as he says, taking both my hands and spreading the printouts over the desk, then place my palms flat on the wooden desk. The anticipation of his touch is torturous. My mind contradicting my heart and sexual desire. Pressing his groin against my arse he leans forward.

Slightly, running his fingers up my bare thighs. He sends shockwaves through my body. Right to the core of my being. Sliding his fingers agonisingly slow between my thighs, he raises them higher and higher until he gets close to the sweet spot. The moment they reach where he needs to be, he curves his fingers into the back of my thong, pulling it down.

"Fuck," I hiss, fisting the paper under my hands.

"You're fucking soaked," he chuckles from behind me as he runs a finger between my wet slit. "Have you been waiting for my touch?"

"Yes," I respond and it's barely even a murmur. "You said this could never happen again." As soon as the words sail out in to the open, I feel him smack my pussy hard. Shoving a single thick digit deep inside me to the knuckle.

"Oh god," I cry out. Reaching back, desperately to touch him any way I can.

"Hands on the fucking table, Ashley. I won't tell you for a third time," he grinds out. My palm slaps against the wood and he begins to laugh. Instantly his finger vacates the space inside me, and I whimper at the loss.

"Nathan. Please," I drop my head. "I'm begging you. Please fuck me." I remember the look on his face the moment I started to beg him for everything I wanted that night.

The silence is deafening and the moment I'm about to turn around, I yelp as he pushes his cock inside me, stretching me open in one single, hard thrust. His hand wraps round my mouth and nose.

"Quiet, love." I nod profusely and he releases my face. "Jesus." *Thrust.* "Fucking." *Thrust.* "Christ." He growls each word with an unrelenting thrust as his thighs slap against mine. "So fucking tight," he growls again. "Look at you taking every inch of me so fucking well."

"Don't stop," I beg, leaning down onto my forearms. Palms still flat on the shiny mahogany surface. "Fuck, you're stretching me out."

My nipples strained against the cotton fabric of my white crop top. With every thrust he assaults on my cunt, they rub against the wood at a delicious angle. I stifle a cry as he shoves a finger in my asshole and I automatically push back because even though it burns, fuck me the sensation of him inside both of my holes makes me drip with desire.

"Gooood girl. Think you can take more?" My eyes flash to my watch and there's ten minutes left.

Ten minutes before hundreds of students flood this place and see me bent over his desk with a finger up my arse and his dick in my cunt. "Has anyone ever fucked your arse before, Ashley?"

The words flowing so effortlessly from his mouth as he continues to fuck me like I mean nothing to him. The way his cock feels sliding in and out of my walls as I Kegel each time he pulls out. Sucking him right back into me.

"N-no," I stutter. Again, more lies. The sound of him spitting onto the place where his finger pierces me, does nothing but make the butterflies in my chest and the wet sounds coming from my cunt work in unison to create the most electric sound. "Yes!" My asshole instantly welcoming a second finger with a deep groan bellowing from his chest as it echoes to the back of the classroom.

"Fuck!" I spit.

"Relax, love. Breathe through the pain and I promise you it will feel so good. Once you're used to three of my fingers, I'm going to shove my cock so deep in your arse you'll feel me for weeks."

"Please, please, please," I beg, I know this is what he likes. What gets him off.

"Please what, Ashley?" He stills and I instantly groan. "Ask me for what you want."

"I need you so bad," I cry out. "Fuck me hard."

"And?" The stillness of his is driving me utterly wild. I try to back up slightly for a tiny amount of friction but when I do, both hands wrap round my throat as he pulls me back at the most impossible angle.

Although my bent fucking spine causes a shoot of pain, I need it. I need the pain. I want to feel something.

"Fuck me like a whore. Hurt me." He smiles down at me, forcing me back down to the table not giving two fucks now if anyone can see us. His aggressive thrusting becomes harsher now, his grunts replacing mine in the room and my eyes begin to flutter closed.

The musical stylings of both our depraved tones dancing together as they bounce off the walls. His free hand slides up my back and into my hair, twisting and knotting itself in there as he uses it to pull me back. Meeting him with every single thrust and the pressure inside me is building exponentially.

I don't know how much longer of this I'll be able to take before I come all over him. Every now and then he smacks my ass so hard it takes me by surprise, and I clench automatically. My cunt is soaking and the wet sounds coming from behind me with each thrust he fucks me up with, is a testament to just what this man does to me.

The fact he's my professor makes this even better. The fact I knew he wouldn't last long before he shoved his fat cock inside me again fills me with delicious delight. But I didn't expect him to crack over paperwork. I have him right where I want him and if I wasn't being railroaded right now, I'd laugh.

This man has absolutely no idea what's in store for him and I fucking live and breathe off it. I can feel myself tightening around him. His cock driving into me without remorse. A loud slap on my ass brings me back to the moment.

"I said don't fucking come." Pulling out of me he grabs the nape of my neck, facing me against the chair. Lifting the latch on the underside of the chair he raises it to its full height and pushes it against the table. "Kneel on it and poke your arse out." I comply with his command. "Keep your fucking mouth shut." As he instantly slams inside of me again and my cry is muffled by his palm cupping my mouth.

Each word he breathes to me, is punctuated with a heavy groan. His body covering me from behind, he spanks me. The tingle of each slap against my ass releases a painful kind of pleasure that I never expected to enjoy. My eyes roll to the back of my head.

"Fuuuck!" I gripe. The aggression becoming more and more harsh as he pounds into me. I try my hardest to move a little further away from him but it's no use.

He holds me there and rains down the most deliciously painful assault that I've ever experienced in my life. I need to separate this feeling and remember that I'm here for a reason that doesn't involve this. I need to focus on that and make sure this doesn't turn into something it doesn't need to be. He pulls out of me, causing me to wince at the loss of him inside me. Nathan grabs my forearm and drags me roughly to the floor. Placing me on my knees as he looks down at me with a disgusting grin on his face.

"Open your whore mouth," he demands, slapping me clean across the face, the sting ringing within my ears, and I can't help the grin that forms. I open my mouth as wide as it will go.

"Be a good girl and poke out your tongue for me." Almost dislocating my jaw in the process. I widen it as far as it will go and seductively flatten my tongue as I press it out. He fists the top of my hair, fucking his fist a few times before an animalistic groan leaves his mouth and warm cum coats my tongue. Crouching down, he grips the nape of my neck, closing my mouth for me.

"Fucking swallow it." Yanking my hair at the back of my neck, my throat bobs as I swallow every bit of his seed. The warm, thick liquid flowing down the back of my throat in quick succession. I open my mouth and poke my tongue out for a second time, just to prove to him that I did what he asked.

"That's my girl." Pushing me away from him, he stands up tucking himself back into his black trousers while I readjust my clothes and thong. Pulling the compact mirror from my purse and checking my face and hair.

Jesus, I look freshly fucked.

"You'll see me after class, Ashley," he whispers as the first students begin to enter the class. Far too busy to look up from their mundane conversations.

"Yes, Sir." The moment the words leave my lips he immediately looks at me with what seems to be pride. Too bad he doesn't hear the thoughts running though my head right now.

I saw him after class, and he made me come so hard I nearly blacked out. Considering I didn't come before the students came into class, he made sure that this time was all about me and I must say, I came three times. Who'd have thought I'd be down for a little degradation and orgasm denial. I have things I need to do while I'm here, I can't afford to get distracted, and he is just that.

It didn't take very long for him to have me squirting all over his desk. However, it's precisely why I'm bounding through the schoolyard to make it to Mia's cheerleading session and also where I will try out for the team. I don't want to, but it's the only way I'm going to get to where I need to be. To seem normal to the others. This really isn't my fucking scene.

At all. She asked me to try out for the team after I showed her a few of my gymnastic competitions where I won first place. Mia thought it would be a great idea for me to join, to get me socialising more. I don't need to fucking socialise. I hate people at the best of times, and I really don't care for much anymore. Yet, here I am, running across the field like a woman possessed. I've had no time to shower or change. I'm just running across the courtyard to the football field with his cum fucking dribbling down my leg and the thought alone causes me to burst out laughing.

This was not on my bingo card for 2023.

Considering he just broke all the rules possible as a teacher, I don't care, it's still not enough. He's professionally fucked up my pussy though that's for sure. I run through the chain fence, ramming it with my shoulder as I pass.

"I'm here!" I shout, waving my hand as I make my way over to Mia and the group of girls that she's standing with that all resemble the flock of seagulls from Finding Nemo. They turn to face me simultaneously as they say *'Mine.'* Ok, well they don't exactly say that, but they might as well have. I'm fucking sweating in this heat. Mia screams as she runs over to me, pulling me into a tight hug, then jumping back in humorous disgust.

"Eww, sweaty."

"I know. I'm so sorry I'm late." I drop my backpack by the bleachers, dragging the cycle shorts from the zip and pulling them on. "I had to run some errands before I came here."

Lie.

Crouching down, I take a seat and rest my feet on the bench in front of me. "I was kept late after class with Professor Danvers. He needed specific pages scanned over to students for class tomorrow."

Another lie.

"It's fine you can-"

"It's not fine." I look up and into the eyes of a redhead as she glares down at me. Her lip curled up as though I'm a piece of shit on her perfectly white

Stellarlyte Kaepa's. "I expect you to be on time to my try-outs." She looks me up and down. Oh, I see. This is the bitch I'm going to be having constant issues with.

"We were late starting because you were late, and we then proceeded to wait around for you to finally show up. Lateness won't be tolerated here." She narrows her eyes at me and sniggers.

"Of course, I'm sorry," Mia nods. God, this girl is sickeningly sweet for her own good.

But it's not my place to step in.

"If you're going to look like that every time you show up for practice, don't bother coming."

I'm sorry. Is this bitch serious.

"Excuse me?" I stand up, tightly grasping the spandex shorts.

"Ashley..." Mia holds my wrist.

"Mia, it's not fine. She's talking to you like shit."

"Don't show up if you can't show out," the redhead chuckles in my face.

"Mia, I will break her fucking nose if you don't tell fire crotch to watch her mouth." I smirk as I see Mia's eyes widen from beside me. I take a step forward and square my shoulders. "Watch your fucking mouth when you talk to me because I… Am not the one."

"There are plenty of girls who want this spot, Ashley," she rolls her eyes. "I've seen your skills and they're sloppy at best. With some training and some control, you could be great. A second to Mia," she shrugs. There's absolutely no conviction in her words. She's saying this because she wants to win. And to win competitions, you need to have the best team put together.

"What a backhanded compliment," I huff.

"Ginger, please, it's my fault." Mia takes the blame for nothing. I'm not taking this shit from her. I'll find another way. Bending down I grab my backpack and place it over one shoulder.

"Ashley." Mia grabs my wrist, looking up at me with pleading eyes and God, fucking damn it I'm a sucker for begging. "Please?"

"You have five minutes to make your decision, Ashley. After that, get the fuck off my field." Fire crotch spins on her heel, her ginger hair almost hitting me in the face as she does. The things I fucking do for you, Maisy. I curse myself.

"She's trying out, Ginger. Just… give us a sec," Mia smiles, pulling me a little from the group. "Ashley, please. This would be so much fun for you, for us."

"Mia," pinching the bridge of my nose, I sigh. "I swear to god if this fucks up my classes or-"

Mia jumps up and down smiling. "It won't I promise." She begins clapping furiously. The excitement seeping out of her pores as she finally stops jumping. The moment I pull on my cycle shorts, she grabs the hem of my skirt and yanks it down while I pull my top over my head.

"Let's go eat after," I wink at her. "You're buying," I point. Mainly because I know this is going to be gruelling and I just can't be fucking assed.

I don't even make it a few steps as all the football players bound onto the pitch for practice.

"Who's the new girl, Mia?" One of them calls.

"Nobody that's interested in you, Marcus. Trust me," Mia calls back over her shoulder.

"Don't have to be interested in someone to fuck them," he calls.

"Are all the guys here like this?" I don't look at Mia when I ask the question. I watch Marcus walk backwards with a smug look on his face. A look that screams out to the world 'I'm a total cocksucker.'

"He does it to all the girls unfortunately." Mia stands next to me crossing her arms. "Just ignore him."

"No." Maybe teaching him a little lesson will help him make better decisions in the future. "No, I don't want to." The humour that weaves through his voice makes my throat fill with lava. I swing round on my heel with the perfect idea springing to mind. I pace over to him in the sexiest way I can muster up. Swaying my hips from side to side. I ignore as the one aptly called Ginger calls my name.

However, the best part of selective hearing is that, if I want to ignore people who talk to me, I can. It's like asshole day at the park and I've been waiting for someone to piss me off.

"Marcus, right?" I know men like him, and they love easy women. I glide my eyes down the entire length of his body, taking in every single aspect of his frame. Sizing him up specifically to see if what I want to do, can be done. The moment my eyeline meets his dick, I grin. Looking up at him I bite my lip.

"See something you like?" he chuckles.

"Actually, I do." I step closer to him, pressing both palms to his chest as he watches me like a hawk. "Always remember to wear your groin guard," I whisper seductively. Why are football players so cocky?

"Speak a little louder I can't-" I don't give him a second to finish before I raise my knee between his legs, crying out as he hits the deck. Crouching down to his level, I watch as he rolls in pain, both hands cupped between his legs, crying out like a little bitch.

"I wouldn't fuck you if you were the last man on earth, and we had to repopulate the world!" All the other players burst out laughing as I walk backwards, lifting both my hands and flipping him off. Turning back to the rest of the cheer team, I notice they're all holding their stomachs and laughing hysterically.

All except the captain. This is a means to a perfect ending. Mia is the only one standing there with her mouth agape. If she's not careful she'll end up catching flies. Walking over to Mia, I place my hand gently under her chin and push up, closing her mouth as she stares at me. Throwing a quick wink her way, I turn to face the team and paint my face with the perfect smile. Again.

"I'm ready when you are," I announce. Making my way to the front of the line as all the girls take their places. Still laughing under their breath as Ginger begins to shout orders.

ASHLEY

Spoiler alert…
I made the team. Obviously. I mean not to blow my own trumpet, but I'm really good at gymnastics. After hitting every call Ginger made, she finally gave in after the girls convinced her to accept me. At one point I thought I'd be late for class, but I managed to shower, get changed, eat, curl my hair, *and* make it to class -Psych 101 with Miss Emerson- all with ten minutes to spare.

Everything relating to academics has always come very natural to me. I've never really had to spend hours studying or looking through things to gain an insight, I'm just lucky. I read something and it just sticks. Having a photographic memory really does do wonders when you need to remember something. It's why I remember Maisy's list. I remember what she wrote, how she wrote it and *exactly* who she named on it.

It's the main reason I'm here. To find out exactly what happened. Dropping down into my seat, I wince slightly. My pussy is still throbbing from the battering I received earlier. That man really doesn't give a single fuck about being gentle. I wiggle in my seat, trying to find a more comfortable position.

"Ok class can you all open your books to page 95." Turning to the white board she begins to write in big letters while she continues. "Today we are going to discuss the Gardner's Theory of Multiple Intelligence and end with the Theory of Dissociative Identity Disorder."

Opening my note book, I grab my tabs and highlighters from the inner zip of my backpack and begin to write. If there's one thing I love, it's making sure all my work from each class is perfectly written with colour coded text and tabs to match. I like everything neat and tidy. It's one of the things that I've always smiled while doing.

The door to the class is yanked open and I immediately look up.

"Sorry, I'm late, Professor, training ran longer than expected." *He* walks in, closing the door politely.

"Just take a seat Jesse, you haven't missed much." She doesn't look at him as she continues to make bullet points on the board for when the discussion begins. Focussing back on my notebook I groan internally as Mr All-American makes his way towards me, eyeing the vacant seat next to me at the back of the class.

"Well, well. Look what we have here," he whispers softly as he drops into the seat.

"There are other seats available for you. Seats away from me." My words coming out impartial and unbothered.

It's how I need to be.

Stay calm Ashley.

Except I am bothered. Inside I'm raging. It's taking everything for me to stay calm right now. I sit back here so I don't have to speak. So, I can listen, take notes, and study what needs to be done. Alone and unnoticed. Just the way I like it. The fact that I already know enough about this asshole already says something.

I didn't come here unprepared. I didn't wait until I knew I was accepted to Brown. I made *sure* I was. In every single way possible. I made sure I knew everything I needed to, about everyone. He just wasn't supposed to notice me yet. But I guess kicking one of the players in the football team was quite a big gesture on my part. This wouldn't be the first time I've put my foot in it when it comes to sculking through the halls like a ghost.

Fuck.

"Why would I want to sit next to anyone else when you're right here. Ripe for the taking," he winks as I look at him, disgust written everywhere on my face. Rolling my eyes, I turn to focus my attention back towards my notepad as Professor Emerson's voice fills the room again.

"Psychodynamic Theorists believe that the effects of Dissociative Identity Disorder, D.I.D for short, results from continuous exposure to traumatic experiences earlier on in life. Most of these include but are not limited to, child abuse, neglect, and parental abandonment." Crossing her arms, I watch as she walks around her desk, leaning on the front. Scanning the room, she continues.

"Can anyone give me examples on the types of identities that might play a large factor within the disorder and what they're specifically there for?"

I feel the chair shift next to me as Jesse leans over. "Do you have a spare pen?"

"Did you not think to come prepared to class," I counter. There's no way this asshole needs a fucking pen. He has a GPA to match mine.

"I forgot my stuff." I don't need to look at him to hear the smile as he speaks. Wrapping my fingers around a blue pen, I offer it to him. Still refusing to look at him as I continue to work.

"There's always a protector," one girl says from the lower levels of the classroom."

"Go on," Professor Emerson pushes.

"The protector is usually the second alter in command, I guess. The one who tends to push forward when the host is experiencing something that reminds them of a traumatic incident."

"Good." She turns back to the white board and writes the word *Protector*. "Anyone else?"

"Each alter will always hold a different memory, role or meaning within the hosts system. Some try to erase the memory altogether. While some are there to help the host cope with the trauma."

Professor Emerson looks up at me in surprise. Her eyes softening as the corner of her mouth begins to quirk up. "Nice of you to join us, Ashley." She pauses, thinking for a second. "Tell me, what would a child alter give someone with D.I.D?"

"A child alter is there to relive childhood experiences that the host never had a chance to participate in. For example, fun, happiness, enjoyment. To experience life through the eyes of a child, if you will. Most of the time alters will also know about themselves and allow others to come forward, when necessary."

She turns to face the board and begins to write. "And what is a necessity for another alter to push through? Anyone else." Releasing a heavy breath, I continue to write.

"Well, well, look who's all smart and shit," Jesse chuckles from beside me. "You think you could tutor me?"

Still not looking at him, I scoff. "You have the same GPA as I do dipshit. You don't need me to school you in Psychology."

"Stalking me I see." Leaning back in his seat, he widens his legs just enough, so his knee rests against mine.

"Your stats are everywhere in this school," I turn to face him again. "I don't need to look you up. Now can you shut up so I can learn. Some of us don't have a full ride scholarship and rich parents."

"Ouch," Jesse clasps his chest in feigned upset. "It's not my fault my parents are rich," he whispers as he leans in closer to me. I lean back away from him the moment his breath tickles the skin on my cheek. I need to get away from this asshole before I stab him to death with a blunt pencil. Just the sight of him makes me sick. As I said before, I know who he is, I've researched him too.

I know everything there is to know about this guy and everything there isn't. His family have covered all of his personal life up but if you pay someone enough, they will divulge anything about anyone. Hackers really are amazing when you get to know them. They can find out all kinds of gruesome little things when it's been redacted.

"I think you-"

"You think?" I cut him off. "That must hurt." I close my books and begin to pack my things away. "Personally Jesse, I have neither the time nor the energy to speak to you. I'd rather gouge my eyes out with a spoon."

"Miss Porter is there a problem?"

All eyes turn to face me as I look around the room. "No Professor, it's just hard for me to hear back here with the continued talking coming from the dipshit next to me." The class hums with chatter.

"Alright class, quieten down, please." She looks between me and Jesse, her lips pursed. "There's a free seat right in front, feel free to take that." She points and I begin to squeeze my way through the aisle.

"Thank you," I nod. I take the few steps down to the front of the classroom and park myself next to what I'm assuming is one of the smart ones. Considering his notepad looks exactly like mine, I smirk. Plonking myself down in the chair I open it up and turn to him. He looks at me, then down at my notebook and smiles softly.

"Nice notebook," he whispers, his pen tapping the page.

"Nice penmanship," I nod towards his writing. He gives me a tight smile and we continue to work in unison. The class goes ahead without a single disturbance, and I couldn't be happier. I might be here for revenge but that doesn't mean I won't be making the most of my time here. However, Jesse now noticing me makes me feel all giddy inside. My unexpected actions worked better than I thought. and pushed everything further along. If there's one thing I know about him, it's that he doesn't take no for an answer.

———— ∘ ✦ ∘ ————

Mia sits at the vanity desk applying her makeup. She seems to think I'm attending this ridiculous party at OBK tonight. Little does she know I have a date with Dracula.

"Can you hurry up we have to leave soon."

"I'm not going to a frat party. Especially the frat house of the guy who's balls I crushed earlier, not to mention Head Bitch will be there."

"Don't tell me you're afraid," she teases. If she knew just how unafraid I was, she'd have me committed. I mean, there's a serial killer roaming university campuses removing the hearts of women he targets, and it's not even filtered into my brain yet that I should be afraid. I can't die yet anyway. Things to do and people to see. She shrugs.

"God damn it," I groan. "Alright, one hour." I hold up a finger and she squeals. "One hour I mean it, Mia, I have a pop quiz tomorrow morning."

"Yeah, yeah. One hour got it," she jumps up from the chair excitedly. "We leave in an hour so hurry up!" She moves my leg over, slapping my bare ass and making her way back over to the chair to finish getting ready herself.

This is going to be dreadful. I hate these kinds of things.

I take my time getting ready and soon enough, I look like a normal human being. Walking from the closet, Mia looks up from her phone and grimaces.

"Uhh, absolutely not." Shaking her head, she reconnects her phone to charge and paces towards me. "There is no way you're wearing that."

I look down at my outfit. "What's wrong with it?"

"It's country looking," she shakes her head. Turning me around to face the full-length mirror. "Can I dress you?"

"You said it was just a few drinks," I slouch in her grasp.

"Honey… It's a frat house. Meaning it's going to be a big party."

"Urgh," I groan. "Fine… Whatever." Mia jumps for joy, running into the closet and rummaging around her side looking for the perfect outfit. I lean over, picking up the image of me and Maisy. Brushing my thumb over her smiling face, I whisper; "I haven't forgotten. I'm just having a little fun. I promise."

"This is it," Mia sings from behind me. As I place the frame back on the table facing my bed I turn around.

"Oh no," I hold my hands up because there is no way I'm wearing that.

"Oh yes!" she squeals yet again, and I fall back onto the bed. "You're going to look so fucking hot in this."

"Mia, I don't want to look hot. I'm going because otherwise you won't stop pestering me." I groan. "Plus, you gave me those ridiculous puppy dog eyes."

"Come onnn," she drones out. Elongating the word into something a stroppy child would say when begging a parent for something they shouldn't be having.

"Stop begging, you look like a dog," I counter. Throwing the towel from my head in her face. She laughs as she catches it and launches the dress at me. "Wear the dress and shut up."

———— ○ ◈ ○ ————

What in the ever-living fuck am I doing? I'll tell you what I'm doing, I'm in a fucking mini dress, walking the streets late at night, to a frat party like my pussy isn't about to drop off with frostbite. Mia convinced me to forgo the coat because it didn't match. The dress I'm wearing is a plain black mini, that sits at the middle of my toned thighs, with spaghetti straps. One move and the girls will fall out. I refused to wear the heels to go with it, so we compromised, and she allowed the Nike Panda's.

"Mia, if I have to walk much longer, I'm calling a fucking Uber. My nipples could cut glass!" I shudder and huddle closer to her as we briskly cross the street.

"Stop moaning. It's right there." She lifts her tanned arm and points to the house at the end of the street.

"Fuck this." I unlink my arm and take off in a sprint.

"Ashley!" Mia shouts from behind me, laughter lacing her voice.

"Hurry up!" I call back to her. The sound of her boots hitting the asphalt behind me as she's hot on my heels. Our giggling melding together as one singular sound. I don't think I've laughed this much in a while. Mia grabs my arm, swinging me around as our laughter becomes even louder.

We stop, leaning against each other to catch our breathe. Mia really has to be one of the most beautiful girls I've ever seen, which makes it unbelievable to me that she's so kind. I take a few steps back dragging her with me.

"Come on we need to-" *Ooof...* The sound leaves my throat as I smack into a hard chest. Looking up, my eyes widen at none other than Nathan standing there.

"Professor Danvers, you're out late," Mia cuts in, pulling me back slightly.

Nathan lifts a 7-11 bag and smiles. "Can't sleep." He looks down on me then, fighting a smirk and throwing my previous words back at him. "Miss Porter."

"Professor."

"You ladies look lovely. Where you heading tonight?" He looks at Mia now, completely ignoring me. I stand there rigid and watch his chest rise and fall. He's not in his usual office wear. Tonight, it's a black Nike tracksuit with Dunks.

"Ashley?" Mia waves a hand in front of me.

"Yeah?" I turn to face her. "Sorry," I laugh. "I totally spaced. I'll meet you inside."

"Ok," she smiles, walking around us and making her way into the frat house.

"Ashley, look at me." Nathan's voice is calm. "Look at me." I tear my eyes from Mia and look directly into his. "About earlier today."

"What about it?" I breathe. Taking a step closer to him, a little too close if I'm honest, my hard nipples brushing along his chest as he groans deep within himself.

"I lost control of the situation."

"Personally, you had full control."

Placing a hand onto my stomach, he slowly takes a step back.

"I made it clear this couldn't happen. My job is important to me. This is all I have; all I've worked for. It's-"

"Ok," I shrug, a tight smile on my face as I walk around him.

"Ok?" He parrots questioningly. I spin on my heel to face him and smile, because there's no fucking way, he's telling me no. I'll play along. For now.

"Yeah," I giggle playfully. "You don't want me that's fine. I won't beg." I take a few more steps backwards. "But you'll crack soon enough."

"Ashley," he growls.

"Miss Porter," I correct him. "I'll see you in class next week." Turning to face the frat house again, I instantly drop my fake as shit smile. I can see by the look in his eyes he wants me. He just needs that little push over the edge, and I have the perfect idea for it. Ascending the stairs into the huge Greek building with large, black Greek letters stuck to the top. The music pumps through my chest, setting the roots of my hair on end.

"Teen drinking is very bad!" Pumps from the speakers as the beat of *Tipsy* by *J-Kwon* blares from the speakers. Red cups raised to the sky as everyone cheers. Bodies grinding against each other as they dance and grind together.

"Jesus Christ," I hate this shit. Why am I even here when I could run into this guy at any other time of the day? The fact I even have to attend this kind of shit just fills me with disgust. I had an idea while getting ready though so it shouldn't be that boring.

Because I'm about to have an entire one-eighty on Jesse. The excitement inside me bubbles up and I fight my hardest to keep that stoic look on my face.

"Not your scene?" I snap to the right and look right into the eyes of Jesse Richmond, head Quarterback, all-American boy, and name number two on my list. I was a little more sold on the idea than I let on, when Mia told me the party was here at Jesse's frat.

"No, this is fun." Sarcasm drips from my words. Mindless drones following the same shit no matter what the year.

He snorts into the red cup before taking a sip of whatever alcoholic beverage rests inside. "You don't do this often, huh?"

"Not at all," I shake my head. His small talk is awful. "How's your friend?" I know Marcus isn't his friend but hey, it's fun to play stupid. He towers over me, watching as he takes another sip.

"My *brother* is fine."

Huh, guess I missed that in my research on him.

"However, he can't play tomorrow's game. Heavy bruising in his nether region."

"Oops," I chuckle.

"We've been telling him for months he needs to wear his guard. Whereas now he will so, I guess… I guess, I should thank you." He taps my shoulder with the back of his hand.

"For kicking your brother in the dick?"

He's silent for a beat. "I guess so."

"You should be fine though."

"Oh yeah? What makes you say that?" he tilts his head playfully, a small wrinkle between his brows.

Focusing back on the people in front of me, I have to hide my disgust. They all knew what was going on.

"I dunno, six-foot-three, two-hundred and ten pounds of," I look back up at him, and clear my throat. Deepening my voice, I recite the stats information I found online. "Lean American muscle with a throwing arm perfect for launching a pigskin from the fifty-yard line."

Pretending to hold a microphone in my hand, I bring my fist close to my mouth. "This gentleman is a strong NFL prospect folks. Twenty-year-old, Jesse Richmond has the ability to withstand hits and go legits."

"Stalker," he says through his laughter. The deep base of the music pumping through the sound system rattles my skeletal structure. What the fuck is with this shit? Jesus Christ. This music really is a crock of shit.

"Nah," I flick my hand between us. "I was bored."

"Ouch." He bends over as though in pain, resting a hand on my shoulder. "And here I thought we were going to be friends."

"Friends?" I scoff. "Guys like you don't have girls as friends. The girls that are your friends are the ones you fuck."

"I'm a good boy, Ashley, I swear," he holds up three fingers in front of me. "Scouts honour."

Another laugh. "There's no way you were a fucking scout."

"You have a pretty laugh."

"Oh god," I groan. "Are you flirting with me? Because if you are it's weak as shit." He takes a step forward and now he's really towering over me. My chest just below his pectoral muscles and I strain to look up at him.

"Nah," he leans down to me. His lips brushing my earlobe as he speaks, and I have to control every action I have to stop myself from fucking puking at him being this close. "If I was flirting, Ash, I'd tell you that I'd love nothing more than to take you upstairs and strip you out of that perfect little dress and fuck what I'm sure is the tightest pussy I've ever had." In an instant he shoots back up and shrugs. "But I'm not. I just think your laugh is pretty."

Gross.

"Let's get you a drink." I don't understand how women could find that kind of talk sexy, the only thing it incites within me is disgust. Most women don't know what he's capable of. Most women aren't me. He takes hold of my hand and leads me through the makeshift dancefloor and my hand burns in his grasp. I'm desperate to pull away, to leave and forget this whole thing, but I can't. I'm here now, I have to see it through.

Stay calm Ashley.

I'm led into the kitchen where the rest of the football team are, Mia's cheer coach Fire Crotch sits on the kitchen side and the moment she notices Jesse holding my hand, her brows furrow and she begins to whisper in another girl's ear. Mia turns around from talking to some guy in the kitchen and looks between me and Jesse, eyes widened but brows furrowed.

"When were you two so… friendly?" Mia leans in and whispers, handing me a red cup filled with what I can only assume is beer.

"Since I kicked his brother in the dick apparently." I take a sip, my lips curling in disgust as I hand it back to her shaking my head. "Eurgh, no, not for me." Stepping away from me, Jesse opens the fridge, pulling out a bottle of ice-cold water and handing it to me with a wink on the end.

"Thanks," I smile. I unscrew the top and take a sip.

"What did Professor Danvers want anyway?" Mia questions as she watches Jesse place his arm back around my shoulder. I'm surprised at her reaction. She's been here longer than me so there's no doubt she knows what he's like with girls.

"Danvers was here?" he looks down at me, screwing his face up in disgust.

What's his problem?

"I bumped into him outside. I'm his TA. He just wanted to run a few things by me before our next lesson," I reply, looking at Mia who's focussed on the arm around my shoulder. I slowly scan the room, noticing more eyes on me than I expected. I'm just waiting for the right moment. If it doesn't happen naturally then I'll make it happen.

"Fuck that guy," Jesse hops up onto the kitchen side. That's when I see her. The brunette with the green eyes. Walking in like she owns the place as her two little cronies follow in behind her. She grabs a cup from one of the other girls and drinks it back in one go. Ginger takes hold of her wrist and I watch as she looks at me while whispering into her ear. I lean between Jesse's legs, propping my forearms up onto his thighs as I dangle the bottle of water from my fingertips. Here we go.

"You don't like him?" Tipping my head back slightly so I can see Jesse.

"Who we talking about?" another guy asks, and I look towards him.

"Danvers," Jesse throws back with venom.

"Yeah, that dude's crazy weird," he takes a sip of his beer. "I heard he's unable to keep his hands off young girls."

"Oh really?" Acting innocent because I know that's a fact. He's fucking me after all, as sickening as it is. But I can't deny he fucks me better than I've ever *been* before.

"I don't see it. He's always been really nice to me," Mia shrugs taking a sip of her drink.

"He just gives off that rapey vibe I guess," the other guy says as he looks at me and frowns. "Oh shit. I just realised where I've seen you from. You're the girl who socked Marcus in the dick right?"

"I guess that's me," I roll my eyes, taking a sip of the water.

"Troy," he holds out his fist and I bump it.

"Ashley."

"Jesse," sings the brunette from beside me as she walks over. "Let's go have some fun." She holds out her hand to him. I look at her hand but refuse to move. Little Miss Francesca Lopez.

New player has entered the game.

"I'm good here Fran. Go find Jacob, I'm sure he's free." Fran looks me up and down in disgust and I do everything I can not to sock her in the mouth. I didn't want to be in this fucking university in the first place. But with everything that's happened, with the things I found out after the fact, that's why I'm here. The quicker I get this over with, the quicker I can move on. The quicker *we* can move on.

"He'll be back when he's bored, honey." She narrows her eyes at me. Her sickly-sweet valley girl accent sings through the air. Making me wonder how the fuck she got into a school like this. She sounds like a fucking idiot. Clearly daddy paid for her to be here.

"The difference is I won't allow him to." I look at my nails. If she's going to accuse me of something, I might as well play into it.

"Won't allow him to what?" she huffs crossing her arms and looking at me confused as hell.

"Get bored." I stand up straighter, looking her dead in the eyes. Ready to taunt her. "Not that I plan on fucking him but," I slide a piece of her hair through my fingers as I lick my bottom lip. "I might just *let* him fuck me in the ass for fun." A slow grin creeps up my face. "Then we'll find out just *who* he's going to keep coming back to. Me, or your raggedy ass snatch." Ending the sentence with a wink. I notice the room go eerily silent as I lean back into Jesse.

"You little bitch!" She lunges for me, I lift my leg up, pressing the sole of my trainer to her stomach as I lean in and smack her with my free hand. She grabs onto my ankle, yanking me from Jesse's hold and down to the floor with her. I drop the water bottle as my ass hits the tile floor of the kitchen with a thud and I swear I've broken my tailbone.

All the while, I'm hysterical with laughter. Watching her rage out is hilarious to me and the fact that women do this over men on a regular basis confuses me more than it should. Why fight over something so insignificant? Rolling on top of me I grab onto her wrists and continue to laugh.

The blood from her nose coating the top of her lip, and her once white teeth are now covered in red. Droplets of blood splattering my chest and face. She manages to slip a hand free, and I brace myself for the hit. She slaps me clean across the face and I feel the moment my lip splits. Both the girls who came with Fran stand there, clapping and cheering as we fight.

"Fucking whore!" she screams.

I continue to laugh. "That all you got?"

"Shut up!" She screams again. I push her back slightly, grabbing onto her hair and dragging her to her feet as I get to mine. Pulling my hand back as far as it will go, I lean into it and slap her round the face just like she did to me. She pirouettes and hits the kitchen counter.

Everyone in the kitchen is chanting *'Fight, fight, fight!'* Brushing the blonde hair from my face I prepare myself to go again but I'm instantly hoisted up and thrown over Jesse's shoulder.

"Jesse, put me down," I continue, howling with laughter. "Let me beat that bitch's ass!"

"Watch when I see you next bitch!" Fran calls. I look up and flip her off with both hands, laughing hysterically.

"Not if I see you first!" More laughter comes now because she has absolutely no idea how true that statement resonates. All this pent-up aggression flows from my body and that was just the beginning. I'm just getting started with the havoc I'm about to cause here. The lives I'm about to ruin.

But you weren't there when she really needed you, Ashley.

"I can walk y'know," I deadpan. Pushing thoughts of Maisy from my mind.

"You can fight too it seems," he counters. "Quite the little mongoose."

"That wasn't nearly enough." A bedroom door opens behind me, and I'm dropped to my feet. I wipe my mouth with the back of my hand and wince.

"Let's get you cleaned up," he says, pulling me into the bathroom, wrapping his hands around my waist, he hoists me up effortlessly onto the bathroom counter. Bending down, I watch as he pulls the first aid box from the small cupboard under the sink, placing it on top of the counter. I love this image he's trying to pursue, trying to convince me and everyone else of. That he's the good boy, when in actual fact he's the sewage line that runs through this entire place.

"I'm fine you know."

"I can't have you bleeding to death." He tears the top of a small plastic packet and removes the antiseptic wipe.

"Dramatic," I state as he takes hold of my chin and runs the wipe over the cut. I hiss, wrapping my hand around his wrist and pulling out of his grasp. "Ow!"

He clicks his teeth, pulling me closer to him again. "So dramatic," he sniffs, throwing my previous words back at him. He works silently. Cleaning my lip as much as possible. I doubt it's even that bad, but I allow him to do it, so he feels like a saviour.

"Why are you being so nice? What's the catch?"

"There's no catch. There's nothing wrong with being nice to someone."

Bullshit.
This good boy persona is a crock of shit.
He'll find out that I know more about him than he thinks.

"Who was the girl downstairs?" I ask, wondering if he'll tell me. Wondering if he will give up the reason why they're not together anymore.

"Jealous?" he asks, picking up the few bloody pieces of tissue and throwing them into the trashcan beside me. I'm incapable of feeling anything that doesn't involve rage.

"You wish." I already know who she is. I just need him to confirm it for me.

"My ex."

One down.

"Recent?"

"Finished last year."

Second down.

"I caught her fucking someone else."

"That's rough. Anyone I might know," I breathe out, laughing on the end of it.

"Professor Danvers."

Ok, I didn't expect that one.

"How the fuck is she still here?" God, I'm better at playing dumb than I thought. I almost convince myself that I am.

"Francesca's father is a big-time donator to the university and well, I was told to keep quiet. And Danvers, well he was told to stay as far away from her as possible."

Bingo.

This is exactly what I wanted to hear. Even though Maisy didn't mention him by name, she did in fact state that Fran was sleeping with someone other than Jesse. I just didn't expect it to be Nathan.

"Does anyone else know what happened with them?" I ask even though I know the answer.

"Why?"

"Just asking," I shrug. "I can warn her off for you if you like?" I laugh, quickly trying to change the subject. Widening my legs, I loop my fingers into his jeans. The hem of my black dress ruching further up my thighs. He places his palms on either side of me, trapping me on the spot.

He doesn't resist me at all and falls into place so easy, like he's always belonged there. I hate what I'm doing right now. I hate knowing that someone who hurt my friend is going about their day like it doesn't matter.

It's like they don't care about anything but themselves. Well, I'm about to change all of that. I'll make them understand. I'll make sure everybody sees what they did.

"What are you doing, Ash?" he clenches his jaw, his eyes scanning over my chest as he talks. I scoff internally because, men, they're all the same. A little attention and they can't help themselves. Give them an inch and they take a mile, give them nothing and they take it all.

"Saying thank you," I shrug. "But if you're not-" I don't get to finish the words before he's on me. Devouring my mouth like it's the last one he'll ever taste. I slide my hands under his black t-shirt and push higher until he pulls it off his body. I have to swallow the disgust in my chest, as his lips find mine again.

His tongue twirling and sucking around mine. He slides his hands roughly up my legs and I have to do everything possible not to throw up in his mouth. He bunches my dress up around my waist, breaking the kiss. Looking down as he widens my legs.

"Up," he smiles, I lift my ass off the side, and he rips my thong from my body.

Just breathe Ash, you can do this.

Placing his hands on the insides on my knees he pushes further and further until my legs burn with how stretched they are. I don't want this, but it's a necessary evil to get to where I need to be. Without this, I can't win. I need to see how far he will go; I need him scared. Panic stricken as he wonders what I'll do.

"Jesse," I breathe seductively. "Eat my pussy." He sucks in a breath, crouching to the floor and immediately spitting directly onto my cunt. I'm allowing the asshole who helped ruin Maisey's life touch me with the same hands that hurt her.

The same person who helped turn her into someone I didn't even recognise. I'll be able to stop him before this goes any further than I want, I just need to see how far he will go. Flattening his tongue, he begins eating me out like a man starved.

It's sloppy at best and I have to fake every single moan. It's depressing that some guys really have no idea how to eat pussy. Yet will expect even a virgin woman to suck a dick correctly.

"Yes, oh my god, yes." I moan out worthlessly into the bathroom. Does he even know what it sounds like when a woman enjoys sex? Because I'm guessing, if he did, he would know this was the fakest shit he's ever heard. He jumps up from the floor, dragging me off the side of the counter and flipping me over. The way he's holding me is bruising, tight and unrelenting. Hold on.

"Jesse," I giggle. "I didn't say you could fuck me." Hoping he will come to his senses and stop, but knowing he won't.

"You sure about that?" he breathes into my ear as I hear the buckle from his belt rattle.

"This isn't funny, Jesse, I said no."

Keep going Jesse.

"Beg me to stop," he growls, the zip ringing as he yanks it down. Pressing my palms to the counter, I push back, trying to turn my body to face him.

"Jesse… I said stop." I press further, but he's stronger than I anticipated. "I-I don't like this, Jesse." With a single thrust he fills me. My cry dancing around the room as he thrusts to the hilt. Tears pool in the corners of my eyes. I didn't want him inside me. He releases a groan as he begins violently pumping into me, running his hands up my back, he grips my throat and yanks my head back.

"Keep going, Ashley," his voice heavy and gravelly.

"Jesse. Stop." *Nothing.* "Jesse, can you hear me I said stop!" He continues thrusting into me, harder and harder. My pelvic bone hitting the handles of the cabinet I'm bent over and the bile in my chest rises.

"JESSE!" I scream. "Get off me!" Snapping my head back, my occipital bone connecting with his nose. The swift sound of a crack hits my ears as he falls back. Pulling my dress down as I turn around and watch him sliding down to the floor. Cupping his nose.

"You broke my fucking nose bitch!" he bellows. Blood spilling out of his nostrils down to his mouth and chill.

"I told you to fucking stop!" I scream back. Kicking him in the legs hard as I can, he cries out and grasps his thigh. "Fucking cock sucker!" Stumbling out of the bathroom I run out of his room and down the stairs. Pushing my way through the bodies of drunken and sexually starved people. I can't fucking breathe.

I need to get out of here.

THE SHADOW

The muffled sobs of the woman in the seat beside me are beginning to grate on me. I haven't even touched her yet and already she has snot dribbling from her bloody nostrils. I groan, dropping my head back against the headrest of the car seat. I swivel my body to face her, and she flinches.

"Listen, Jules… can I call you, Jules?" *Nothing.* "Perfect. Now, your voice, is reaaally annoying. I gagged you for a reason and that reason is so you would shut the fuck up. Anyone would think you're about to die." I pause. She pauses. Both of us just staring at each other for what feels like eternity. "Come on." I wiggle my eyebrows. "That's funny." I search her face for any kind of reaction. Instead, she just starts screaming even louder.

Thrashing around in her restraints, like that's going to help her. I'll let you in on a little secret… it's not. Her eyes shut tight as the tears fall from the corners and bleed out onto her dirt-stained cheeks. Wriggling in her restraints.

"Jules you won't get out of this." I groan, her screaming filling the car. "Jules." If she carries on, she'll get us caught and I don't want our little date to come to an end so fast. "SHUUUT UP JULIET!" I scream, punching her square in the face and breaking her nose in the process. Her head snaps to the left and she's out like a light. Blood has splattered the car interior.

"Look what you did!" I shout, punching the dashboard a few times to get my anger out. "God. Fucking. Damn. It!" I punch the hard plastic with every single word.

Taking a deep breath, I release it slowly and turn back to face the steering wheel. I really need to calm down. My therapist tells me I'm doing well with my anger issues, and I plan on keeping it that way for the foreseeable future. This isn't how I intended to spend my evening but well, here I am. Sitting in the car thinking about the woman I've now apparently become obsessed with.

The one next to me is just a filler, until I can find the right time to make my move. This is the second woman in a week. I'm never usually this desperate for another woman so close to the last. I'm parked in the forest just by Institute Woods. It's late at night and I'm very close to home. I drove her here after I managed to convince her to let me take her home after our date.

I never operate this close to a well populated area either but as I said, I was desperate. I pull the latch on the car door, using my foot to kick it open because I'm fucking pissed right now. I could be watching my blonde beauty but I'm here with this mess. There's one girl I want, but it's too fucking soon so, yet again, I have to deal with this wretched cum bucket. This new girl, she's perfect. Innocent and bubbly on the outside but I know exactly what she is.

I see her when she thinks nobody else is looking. She is completely out of my league and not my type. Where I usually go for brunettes, this one is a perfect blonde with the biggest fucking tits I've ever seen.

She's phenomenal in the looks department too. I'm not into cannibalism, but I think I'll save that heart. I jog the few steps round the hood of the car and yank the passenger's side open. Jules slumps to the side. I lean in and press the clip on the seatbelt, and she falls to my feet with a thud.

"I really have to do everything myself," I groan, sliding my hands underneath her arms and dragging her back against the treeline. She's not struggling now, which thankfully means I can do what needs to be done. Nothing worse than being interrupted when you're trying to get shit done. I'll wake her up soon enough and then we can both join in on the festivities of the evening.

I drop her down at the base of the tree and her head smacks against the large tree root sticking out. "Sorry, Jules." Jogging back to the car I pop the trunk and wrap my hand around the leather-bound surgeon's bag and slam the trunk shut.

Making my way back over to the little sleeping princess. I position her the way I want, then begin to unbutton the college cardigan she's wearing. Now, let me explain something, I wasn't born this way. I'm not like the typical serial killers that are born fucked up. I didn't torture poor animals on my way to the top. I didn't like to sift through dead animal carcass like Dhamer.

I've never and I mean NEVER skinned someone to make a fucking lampshade either. That's some fucking sick shit. I just kind of woke up one morning and y'know, felt like killing someone. My first time was eighteen. Hitchhiker by the name of Angelica Jones and boy was she beautiful. I was driving home late one night, and I saw her walking backwards down a dark road with her thumb sticking out.

This isn't the usual thing to see where I'm from, there was no one about and I was curious, so I stopped. I strangled her on a dark road exactly thirteen minutes after I picked up. Her beautiful green eyes widened the moment I knew she was about to take her last breath. Some of the blood vessels had already popped in the whites of her eyes.

I was relentless. Long strands of brunette hair stuck to the sweat on her face as the light in her eyes died out. Then, I sat there. Watching and waiting for something to happen. Some kind of fucking miracle that she would wake up and I could do it again. Spoiler alert, she didn't. It was over far too quickly for my liking, and it was then that I learnt I had to be patient. Take things slow.

Make a woman feel good before I end her life for pleasure. It's like then you're engaging in self-pleasure, you don't just go all the way in and start bashing the snake like a madman -some people do, but I like taking things slow- you have to work up to the crescendo. Learn patience and make time your ally. I could never bring myself to fuck her corpse though. I get the appeal, I guess. They don't move, don't fight and you can just pump away without having to ask them if they're ok.

Once I read you can catch some form of dick rot when you fuck dead bodies, true or not, I was *never* taking that chance. The cops call me a serial killer, I'm not. I'm more a man of opportunity. I don't kill all the time, I'm also well aware that what I'm doing is completely fucked up and wrong but it's like the first time you have sex.

No, you guys know the Pringles advert 'Once you pop you can't stop.' That. It really is like that. So many people on this earth claim they can do it, but very few of them can. I take what I need when I need it, and tonight, I needed a fix. Because when I'm done here, I'll go clean up and make my way over to see my blonde beauty. I crouch down beside Jules who's still passed the fuck out, thankfully.

If that's how she sounds when she's being rooted then I think the men, or women, of the world are better off without her. I need to work quickly because as I said, I'm never this close to home. I travel out so I don't get caught. Fingering the hem of the white t-shirt she's wearing I rip it down the middle exposing a pair of perfect tens.

"Jules, who'd have known you had these bad boys underneath and no bra too. Dirty girl." I smirk, smacking one of them. Watching it jiggle left and right. I need to stop fucking around and work. As I was saying, after spending time in the car with my first kill, that's where I developed my desire for killing brunettes. It was nothing to do with my mum being a whore or a terrible home life, it was far simpler than that.

I just liked the way a dead woman with brown hair looked. The colour contrast best suited the imagery I like to remember. I'm not your typical man. I remember every woman I've killed, where I buried them and their names. I remember everything about the scene and will never forget their anniversaries. I'm just a romantic kind of guy.

Sliding the butcher knife from the bag, I slap Jules face a few times until she starts to come through.

"Come on princess, wake up. I need you with me." She groggily rolls her head from side to side as her eyes begin to flutter open. "I need you awake."

I slap her cheek again and her eyes meet mine. "Now listen, I need to make this quick, I have somewhere I need to be so can you please sit still."

Her chest begins to shake as the sobbing takes hold of her. I almost feel sorry for this one. Almost. Raising the knife in my hand I bring it down with such force that it pierces her chest cavity. Her muffled screaming piercing the silence in my mind as I end this torturous date.

I lean over the knife and watch the blood weep from the wound and pool in that little crevice just at the base of the neck. Next, I grab the scalpel and slowly run it from one end of her throat to the other. The realisation finally hitting her that she's never going to make it out of this situation. Never going to make it home. That look. Priceless. I yank the knife from her chest and smile.

I'll let her bleed out while I get ready to remove the heart. Because I like to make things hard on myself, I could do this on an operating table in my basement, but I live in a place where everyone is so fucking nosey, I'd easily get caught. So, I make do with what I have and what I have is a manual bone saw. Throwing the knife and the scalpel back into the bag, I take both ends of the bone saw and get to work.

It's already later than expected and I hate having to rush. I press the blade to the open wound where the knife used to be and begin to move it back and forth.

The sound of bone crunching and grinding against the jagged blade is like music to my ears. Her skin tearing jaggedly as she lays there, letting me work in silence.

By the time I'm finished opening the chest, I'm fucking sweating behind my mask. Rummaging back through my things, I find the rib retractor and squeeze in between her ribcage and begin to wind the small handle. My hard cock is straining against the zip of my jeans the more crunching and snapping of bones fills my ears.

I'm going to fuck myself so hard later.

Her chest is open just enough now, so I wrap my hand on one side, slide my black boot against the other and rip it apart. Blood spitting onto me and I groan in pleasure.

"Jules, you naughty, little girl. You lied. You said you weren't a smoker," I laugh as I look down at her blackened lungs. "However, the hard on I'm sporting right now is all you baby." It's then that I have a thought.

I can't wait.

Moving from the top of her I lay down beside her, looking up at the stars and smiling.

"This will be my first time with you, Jules. You sounded like a fucking foghorn, but I can't take it anymore." With my latex gloves covered in blood I undo the button and zip of my jeans, lifting the elastic waistband of my boxers and wrap a bloodied, hand around my strained and angry cock, working myself up and down.

"Holy fuck, you feel so good." My eyes flutter closed as the still warm blood coats me, giving me the most sensational feeling against the cold night air.

I need more.

Letting go of my throbbing cock, I rummage around in the open guts of Jules and coat my hand in more blood. Reaching back to myself, I stifle a groan and chuckle at the thought of someone seeing me now.

This random fucking guy, fisting himself next to a dead body. Not fucking it though. The thought of someone watching pushes me further over the edge as I work myself harder and faster. My moans bleeding out into the night air to anyone who is close enough to hear. In this moment, I don't care if anyone sees because this is possibly the best wank, I've ever given myself.

"Fuck, fuck, fuck," I chant, lifting up my jumper as thick, warm cum squirts all over my chest. That was a lot quicker than usual. Is blood my thing now?

Hmm, interesting. Research might be needed.

"Sorry about that, Jules. How rude of me. Let me get this sorted and I'll get you covered up." Righting myself and covering my cum covered chest back up, I get to work. Straddling her again.

"Now *that* is a beautiful heart, Jules. You were holding out on me." I grab the scalpel again and begin to delicately slice over each of the arteries I can see. Leaving the carotid till last. That one's my favourite attachment. I get to my feet, still in a crouched position, and wrap both my hands around the muscular organ and in one swift movement, I rip the entire thing from Jules' chest.

Raising it to the sky like Mufasa did when he showed that little asshole, Simba. I pull the medium sized Tupperware box out from the bag and neatly place the heart inside, leaving it placed exactly where I usually do.

"Well, Jules, thanks for the date and the wank. It was mesmerising, to say the least," I laugh as I pack up my belongings. "Thanks for the apparent new kink, too."

Standing up I make my way back over to the car and check my watch.

Right on time.

――― ○ ◈ ○ ―――

I've been laying under her bed for the past hour, waiting for the sleeping tablets to kick in. She really needs to be more careful leaving her window unlocked as well as leaving her water on the bedside table and trusting that it's safe. I'm a depraved bastard and even I wouldn't trust a floor full of women.

That's why I take them one by one, when they're walking alone at night. It's easier. Anyway, I crushed two tablets into her water. Enough to have her sleepy but not enough to have her completely comatose.

The moment I hear her breath level out and her gentle snore fill the room, I know it's time. I'm a big guy, so crunching myself into the foetal position is fucking uncomfortable but I did it for her.

I've been watching her for the past week, and I'd do anything for her. I don't know when I became obsessed with Ashley, but what I do know, is what I see in her.

Me.

I drag myself from under her bed as slowly as I can. I'm not exactly sure when her roommate will be back, so I simply click the lock on the door just to be safe. If anyone saw what I'm about to do to Ashley, I'd have to kill them. Ashley doesn't deserve that right now. After all, the roommate hasn't done anything to piss me off... yet.

I'm surprised I actually got here in time after I had to go home, shower and change. Can't see my girl all messy with someone else on me. I quietly walk over to the double bed, standing above her as I watch her chest rise and fall. The act hypnotising and I find myself caught up in just staring at her. The oversized, grey band t-shirt she's wearing has risen up over her peachy little ass.

Taking the knife from my back pocket, I press the button on the side and flick the blade from its casing. I take a step forward, stilling as the floorboard creaks under my black boot. My eyes going from the floor and back to her.

Nothing.

I slide the tip of the blade up the hem of the t-shirt and lift it, groaning as I realise, she has no underwear on.

"Oh, Ashley," I croon. "What a naughty girl. Were you waiting for me?" Pressing a knee onto the bed, the mattress dips as I make my move to position myself at her feet. I have to touch her; I have to feel her warm skin beneath mine. Pulling the latex gloves from both my hands, I press one to the mattress to balance myself and I slide the other agonisingly slow up her calf.

The moment I reach just above her knee, I curve my fingers round it and softly pull her leg to the side. Her perfect pussy glistening and on show for me. Making my mouth fill with water, I'm barely holding on by a thread. Sucking two fingers into my mouth, I put as much saliva onto them as I can.

"I'm going to make you feel so good, baby. I'm sorry I had to drug you for our first time. But the next time we do, I promise you'll be awake and ready for me." The last word falls into the darkness of the room and Ashley shifts onto her back.

Her foot pressing against my thigh as both her legs fall open now and my god it's like everything I've done in my life has paid off. I'm about to eat the juiciest pussy I've ever fucking seen, and I can't wait. I feel like a kid the first time they realise Santa has been. I'm going to lick every fucking inch of her and when she's wet enough, I'm going to shove my cock so deep in her fucking cunt she will feel me in the morning.

Getting myself into position, I lean in and run my nose up the slit of her pussy, coating it in her juices and taking a deep breath, inhaling the sweet vanilla scent of her shower gel.

"Fuck meee," I groan heavily. I gently bring her legs up, pressing my forearm against the back of her knees and I push back. The movement raising her ass off bed slightly. Leaning in even closer this time, I press my free hand on her ass cheek, spreading it apart to look at her perfectly pink asshole.

Flattening my tongue, I lean in and run it slowly from her asshole to the opening of her tight cunt. A guttural groan vibrates in my chest as my tastebuds ignite with her cum on my tongue. The taste exploding, making my eyes roll back.

"Fuck this. I need you naked, baby."

Lowering her legs, I carefully slide the t-shirt up her perfect body, bunching it in my hands and lifting her head up as I pull it over her. She lays there then; bare as the day she was born, and my cock is straining so tight against my jeans if I move too fast, I'll cum myself. I'm now leaning between her legs, looking down at her awaiting body.

I gather spit into my mouth and let it drop from my tongue, landing perfectly onto her slit. Pressing two middle fingers to her hole, I push in slowly, watching as she groans and arches her back in response.

"That's my girl, you respond so well to me." I begin to finger fuck her, slowly to start because I'm desperate to feel every single groove of the inside walls of her cunt. To feel her clamp down on me as she comes. I keep pumping, watching as her tits move up and down with every single deep thrust I fuck into her.

"Uhh," she groans in her sleep, arching her back slightly. And it spurs me on.

"You like that, baby."

"Mmm," sucking her bottom lip into her mouth. She's enjoying this just as much as I thought she would, but this still isn't enough. I need her to come. Hard. "Fuck me." She whispers groggily, the unexpected words seep out into the fabric of the room and I still. There's no way I heard that right. Moaning she rolls over onto her front, her legs still spread on either side of me. My fingers now removed from inside her.

"Fuck me..." There they are again.

Whatever you want my girl.

Immediately, I pop the button of my black cargos and pull them down with my boxers. I've never wanted to fuck someone as much as I want to fuck Ashley. She's all I've thought about. Reaching to the front of her thighs, I hoist her ass into the air and rub the head of my cock through the juices weeping from her greedy cunt. Her phone lights up on the bedside table with a text, from an unknown number.

"Ashley, you broke my fucking nose!"

And another.

"I'm going fucking kill you!"

Whoever this little cocksucker is, there's no way he's touching what belongs to me. If anyone will kill Ashley, I will. Lining myself up at her entrance I push forward, and the hottest sound comes from her mouth. I can't be gentle; I can't be slow. I begin assaulting her with as much force as I can muster, black spots building behind my eyelids.

Nathan

"*Another body was found last night by Institute Woods, just outside of Brown University.*" The news reporter on the television reads. "*The woman was found in the early hours of the morning with her heart cut from her chest and left by the side of her head. The police suspect the Serial Killer, known as Casanova, is now moving further into the surrounding area.*" Tears well up in the news reporter's eyes, as myself and the students watch clips from police footage. "*Juliet Jones went missing three nights ago from the town of Glen Mills and has been missing until the discovery of her body.*"

I press the button on the TV remote, placing it back on the table and turning to face the class. "So," I lean back against the desk as every student focuses back to me. I try my hardest not to look at Ashley for too long either, the tension between us is utterly palpable and I need to keep that to a minimum in class. "What do we know so far about the person doing all these killings?" A student puts his hand up. "Yes."

"Usually, he leaves the bodies in the town that he kidnaps the women from. So, he's brave. Not afraid of getting caught."

"Maybe a god complex?" The girl next to him jumps in. "Sees himself as untouchable."

"Maybe he wants to be caught." The first student interrupts.

"How so?" I question, clasping my hands in front of me and tilting my head.

"Think about it, he usually kills randomly, in different towns and always the same kind of girl. This one, it was messy, in a forest, close to a university. Maybe he's spiralling."

Ashley scoffs from the front row.

"Something to add, Miss Porter?"

"He's not spiralling nor did something scare him." Her smug little smile causes me to bite the inside of my cheek. She's so fucking sexy, sitting there in a tight white tank, and ripped denim jeans.

Her long, toned legs are stretched out under the table and crossed at the ankle. She's not wearing a bra today, so the peaks of her nipples cause the ribbed, cotton fabric to stretch over each one.

I look at her and smirk. "Explain." Leaning forward onto the desk she rests her forearms on the table. Her breasts pooling to the top of the vest as she speaks.

"Someone like him, doesn't spiral. He's evolving. He dates the women for three weeks, keeps them for three days and kills them on the third day. The women he kills are twenty-one. One plus two is three."

"What's your point Miss Porter?" My tone bored; it will rile her up.

"He has OCD. It's impossible for him to spiral when everything is so meticulous with him. Three cuts to the heart and three stabs to the chest, everything has to be perfect for him. That murder,"

she points to the TV, "he wasn't spooked, he had somewhere to be." The confidence oozing off of her is frustrating me in the best way. "He'll probably start fucking them soon anyway."

"Ok, that's enough." I stand from my desk, walking around to the back to get the papers from my satchel.

"The sick bastard probably fucks himself with their blood or something." She laughs.

"Miss Porter, I said that's enough," I repeat, trying my hardest to stay calm.

"I wouldn't be surprised if he couldn't get it up either. Probably why he's killing young women." She laughs, and the class join in with her.

"Ashley, that's enough!" I bellow, slamming my fist on the wooden desk as the entire class goes still. I watch as the corner of her mouth twitches. Calming myself, I address the class. "There's nothing to say that he has evolved into anything to do with blood. This killer is just like you said. Meticulous at what he does. He doesn't have time to be distracted from murdering women," I scoff. "He leaves absolutely no mess and makes sure all his crime scenes are tidy and easily found by the police."

"Oh, how fucking kind of him," she chuckles. "Making sure the families of these girls find them quick enough."

I pinch the bridge of my nose. She's beginning to get on my last nerve. It's bad enough I have to sit there and look at her sitting in front of me, trying my hardest not to shove my cock so far down her throat she chokes. "Ashley, please stop talking."

"Why?" She stands up, hands on the table.

"Excuse me?" What the fuck does she think she's doing. Trying to push me, undermine me in front of the student body?

"You heard me? You ask us to profile, I profile and what? Is it not good enough for you?"

"Go to my office." I'm done with this. All the students are watching this pathetic argument going on between the pair of us and I'm beginning to lose my temper. Something I never do when working.

"Just because you're stuck here teaching classes instead of being out there," she slams her book closed, "don't punish us for it."

"My office, right now!" I point to the door as I watch her laugh. Gathering all her things together and stomping out of the room. Clearing my throat after I watch her leave, I look towards the class and remove any trace of emotion from my face. "Class dismissed. Chapters eight to nineteen in your textbooks and I want a full breakdown profile for this serial killer and what you think he might do next."

The students begin packing their stuff away and chatting amongst themselves. I shove all my things into my satchel and I'm furious.

Storming out the door, I make my way through the flow of students, willing myself to calm down as much as I can before I get to the office. I never get angry; I never shout and in a few seconds this girl has managed to put me in a mood to fucking smack the shit out of her.

Pushing through the wooden door to the secretary's office, I smile. "Sharon, feel free to go to lunch. I have Ashley Porter in my office for a meeting regarding her behaviour and this could take a while."

"Oh, of course. Is there anything I can do beforehand?"

I smile briefly. "No thank you. Just shut the door on your way out and make sure the busy sign is turned round. I want no interruptions during my session."

"Of course, Professor." She smiles, grabbing her bag as she circles the desk, turns the 'Do Not Disturb' sign over and leaves. I have an hour.

That's all I need. Pushing through the door to my office, Ashley is sitting on the desk cross legged with a grin on her face. She did this on purpose and I'll be sure to punish her for that. She begins to talk but I ignore every single word that comes out of her mouth. Throwing my satchel on the chair next to me, I slam the door behind me, making her flinch. I walk over and grab her tightly by the throat. Pushing myself between her legs, I drag her face to meet mine as I look down at her.

"Did you think that was funny?" The sound of my voice completely fucking enraged. "Do you think that's the best way to get my attention?" Pushing her back and out of my grasp, she sucks in a deep breathe. I watch as she grins, the way she looks at me is addicting, the way her eyes bore into mine, make me harder than I've ever been with a woman before. The fact that she's nineteen has nothing to do with it, and at the same time... everything.

"Take off your clothes," I demand, staring her dead in the eyes. She doesn't move. "Take them off!" I shout, pointing in her face. I move back and watch as she stands in front of me. Slowly unbuttoning her jeans, her stare never leaving mine as she wiggles them down her thighs and they fall to the floor revealing a silk red thong. The wet patch I can see is testament that my behaviour isn't frightening her but turning her on. She pulls her vest up and over her head.

"Sit back on the desk, Ashley, don't make me ask you twice." She immediately complies and I stalk back between her legs. "If you're frustrated and you need to come, then fucking ask me. Don't embarrass me in front of the class."

I turn to the side and step back pressing her right leg to the back of my thighs. I take my left arm and press it against the inner thigh of her other leg, pushing them as far apart as possible.

"I'll make you come, again and again. Until you're a quivering fucking mess on my desk and you're going to fucking take it. Do you understand me?"

"Y-yes," she breathes.

"Spit." Placing my four fingers in front of her mouth, she gathers the spit then opens her mouth for me. I do everything I can to suppress how fucking turned on she gets me. I told her this was never going to happen again. Promised myself that I wasn't going to jeopardise my life here and look at me. Desperate and ready to fuck her at any second. I shove my fingers into her mouth and into the back of her throat till she begins to gag and cough.

"Pull your thong to the side and hold it. Don't move, in fact, don't fucking speak and you only come when I say so. Understand?" She nods swiftly, my fingers still lodged in the back of her throat as I watch her hook her fingers inside the silk fabric, yanking it to the side to reveal those all too familiar pussy lips.

Looking back into her eyes, I remove my fingers, turn my palm upside down and spank her pussy. Her moan fills the room and I smile. Running my fingers up and down through her wet lips I watch as they begin to tint pinker, I press two fingers inside easily and she holds back her moan this time.

"That's my good girl," I praise her, still staring as her eyes flutter the moment I begin to move in and out of her. "You're so fucking wet, love. Is all this for me?" She nods, her pussy juice and spit coating both fingers perfectly.

Pulling them out, I rain down another spank in the same spot as the first. She grits her teeth, hissing at the pain, then groaning in ecstasy as I slide my fingers back in. I curve them up slightly and begin fucking her. The movement of my fingers swift and fast.

Moving my hand up and down to reach that deeply intense pleasure spot. Her heavy breathing falls out in to the open as her mouth forms the perfect 'O' shape, small creases between her eyebrows as she sucks in a deep breath.

"That's my girl. Stay quiet. Unless you want someone in here to watch? Someone to watch me bury my cock into that warm cunt of yours so everyone knows who it belongs to?"

"No," she huffs out. "I just… Fuck, fuck, fuck." I laugh as she chants. She loses her mind in euphoria, as she relinquishes complete control to me.

"You're going to come for me…"

"Yes, oh fuck, yes." Her breathing erratic and her face screwed up as she tries to hold her growing orgasm.

"Right. Fucking. Now." The moment those words leave my lips and I pull out my fingers, a stream of cum squirts out from her. Hitting the chair and my fucking satchel. Rubbing my hand back and forth, I spread it all over her and myself. Luckily, I have a spare suit in the closet. Her once bright red thong is now soaked through, and her chest rises and falls with short pumps.

"Again," I command.

"Nathan, just give me… a second." Her words coming out breathlessly. "I can't-"

"Yes, you can," I grab her throat. "And you will." Reciprocating the same action as previous. More vigorous this time. I press my hand to her mouth to stop her from screaming and she quickly rests her hands behind her for balance, screaming beneath my hand as she comes again.

Squirting all over my shirt. Fuck, she's sexy when she's at my mercy. Turning to face her I wrap both hands round her throat, shaking her once.

"Is this what you wanted?" I slap her, this time in the face.

"Yes," she hums. Pushing her flat against the table, she spreads her legs, thinking I might fuck her in this moment. But this is about punishment. About her coming constantly until it fucking hurts. I leave her laying there, her head moving to follow me. Walking behind my table I look down at her.

"Hang your head off the table, Ashley."

"What are you-" I don't let her finish the words before I slap her again. I yank her forward slightly, making sure she's at the perfect angle. "I'm going to fill that fucking throat up. Unzip my trousers and take out my cock."

As she works the zip on my black work trousers I lean forward and slide my fingers inside her again, fucking her deep and hard with three fingers. She cries out at the invasion, and I smack my hand over her mouth, locking in the sound.

"I said shut your fucking mouth," I whisper-shout. Her eyes widen at my tone, I don't care right now. The only thing I care about is getting caught and right now that's not a fucking option.

Having someone walk in my office, only to see Ashley in one of the most damning and compromising positions of my life, is not... an option. I work her up again, bringing her to the precipice of another orgasm, her back bowing off the table.

"Come for me... Again!" My words grinding out. I work her harder, faster, demanding those orgasms from her because they all belong to me. Her legs shudder and she again, screams behind my hand. Looking at her spread for me on my desk, watching as her orgasm aggressively rolls through her entire body with an intense shudder, it fills me with absolute delight that I have her like this.

Sure, I've tried to ignore the pull I have with her, but I can't anymore. I spend every single waking fucking moment thinking about her. From the moment I go to sleep at night and immediately as I wake up. I just need to make sure it's nothing like last time. I can't have that again.

Removing my hand from her mouth I step closer to her, she wraps her soft, delicate hands around my cock, stroking up and down a few times before she takes it into her mouth. Every single fucking time I'm inside her it's like fucking heaven.

Placing my hand flat on the desk, I lean forward, pressing myself further down her throat inch by inch until the head pokes the back of her throat. Moving back instantly, she clears her throat as the thick string of saliva slides down her cheek.

"More?" I ask and she nods in silence. But I want to hear her saying. "Beg."

"Please, please can I have your cock." She opens her mouth and I shove myself back inside her throat, thrusting in and out until the wet sounds from the buildup of saliva fill the room.

"I can see my cock in your throat, love," I grit out, so fucking turned on by the sight of it. Her throat constricting around my thick shaft feels better than anything I've ever experienced. Well, not everything, but that feeling is different. I'm addicted to fucking Ashley.

I pull back out and she sucks in a deep, agonising breath. Her exasperated breathing just turns me on even more. Jesus, she's perfect. I almost don't want it to end. I wrap my hand around her throat and spin her body around to face me, knocking paper and pens everywhere.

Spreading her legs wide, I line myself up and impale myself into her absolutely soaking wet centre.

"Fuuuck," I growl against her open mouth as her screams of ecstasy spill out into mine. "You feel so tight wrapped around me, love." Gripping onto her thighs, I lift her into my arms and walk over to the small, black leather couch I have by the window.

Nobody can see this high up but there's always a chance and the thought of that scares the shit out of me. This happened before and I had to move schools because of it. Don't ask me why I'm taking my career in my hands like this again because I wouldn't be able to tell you. The only thing I know for sure is that I need Ashley to-

"Move, baby," I moan, dropping my head back onto the seat as she begins rolling her body against me. I watch all her facial expressions as she frowns at the loss of me and then continues to bite her lip every single time she pushes me back inside her. "Just like that, love." Fuck. If she carries on doing this, I'm not going to last long at all. "Fuuuck, yes." I hold her arse cheeks in a vice like grip and control the pace. Needing more. Needing to be deeper.

"Oh my god!" She cries. I don't even care that its louder than usual. I told her to be quiet but the way this feels right now, I've lost all care of someone finding us.

"Play with yourself." I move my hands to her face and pull her closer to me, her forehead resting upon mine. I slouch down from the seat and start pumping and thrusting into her relentlessly as she uses one hand to cover her mouth and the other to rub circles on her swollen clit as I bring her to orgasm.

"Mmm, fuck, oh my god, Nathan. Please, harder."

My love needs it harder.

Wrapping my arm around her waist I flip us over so she's on her back and continue taking my fury out on her. Poundng into her like a man starved.

"Yes… Just like that. Don't stop," she mewls.

"Fuck, Ashley you feel so fucking good," I moan right back.

"Yes, yes, yessss!" She cries out further, her fingers in her mouth as she desperately tries to contain her screams. "Ohmygod, ohmygoddddd!"

The words begin to blend together for her as I lean forward, moving her hips up into a new angle. One that hits that sweet spot. And I can't help the smile on my face as I obliterate any man that's come before me.

"Shh," I laugh through the hushed tone. "You need to be quiet." Her eyes begin to flutter, and she slowly begins to tighten around me.

"You want to come?" I lean down and whisper against her mouth. Kissing her deeply. My tongue battling with hers for control.

"Fuck, I can't... hold it anymore."

"Yes, you can…" Her legs resting over my muscular thighs, I gently hold on to her and begin raining down hard and deep controlled thrusts. Her perfect tits bounding up and down as I go. Pulling out all the way to the tip, then thrusting back in all the way to my pelvic bone.

Only the sound of the leather creaking beneath us as she holds her breath. She says two words then. Two words that send me over the edge.

"Choke."

Thrust.

"Me!"

Thrust.

Fuck, baby, I'll give you exactly what you want. Leaning up straight I wrap both hands around her beautifully slender neck. The tendons raised and pushing through the skin. Her eyes widen for a second as I thrust even harder than before, and I squeeze.

With every single thrust, I squeeze her delicate neck tighter and tighter. Her face turns red, and she explodes all over me, squirting as I pull out and push back in. The front of me is completely soaked, my white shirt turned see through, and I groan as she passes out entirely.

Letting go of her throat I lean over and continue fucking her. Looking down on her as she breathes sweetly, unknowing that I'm still going at her.

It's almost as if she's dead. At that thought I feel my entire body tense up and release everything I've had built up since last night, inside of her. Roaring with the last thrust.

"Holy shit." My breathing comes out in pants, and I begin to laugh. Dropping my head forward and laughing through the heavy breaths. "That's new." Pulling out of her, I sit back on my heals and steady my breath. Looking down at myself, dick hanging out and drenched in her cum, I laugh again. Looks like I can't deny her as much as I thought I could.

Diary Entry, Maisy

November 18th, 2022

What I thought would start as a really good day, turned into Hell on earth. Fran and her minions decided bullying me on a daily basis with words, just wasn't enough. I don't know what the hell I'm still doing here.

My life is practically a living hell. Today, I was showering in the dorms once I thought everyone had returned to their rooms only to be greeted with a terrible beating from Fran. To make matters worse, she's my roommate.

I don't know what I did to get on their radar, and I don't know why I deserve to suffer this daily, but I guess this is karma of some sort. They dragged me from the shower only to cover me, head to toe in a gallon of coke.

After, they proceeded to smack me about between the three of them. I have a split lip and a black eye already beginning to show. I've been allocated a single room by the Dean of Admissions, Joseph Chambers. I finally stopped caring what everyone thought and told him what's been going on.

During the fifteen minutes I spent in his office, he all but told me nothing would be done about Fran unless I gave him something too.

The moment his hand slid over my bare thighs; I knew what he was asking. It was then that I also realised that I was now totally alone. I have nothing and no one to look after me. I've even pushed my best friend away. I need to find a way out.

A way to free myself from all this shit I'm wading through in this school. I've never felt so alone, I've never hated myself more than I do right now.

I'm disgusted that I allowed him to touch me, just so I could have a break from all the pain. The last of my innocence fading away with his touch.

Maisy.

ASHLEY

I lean against the tree and watch as Fran laughs with her friends while crossing the road. The orange tip of my cigarette the only light source. I'm far enough away so nobody notices me, wearing dark enough clothes, I easily blend in with the treeline.

Seems she walks this way home regularly with her stupid airhead friends. Her cackle causes me to grimace. What a fucking rat. I've spent the past three days staying as far away from her rapey ex-boyfriend, Jesse, who must've fucked me a little harder than I thought, because the day after, my pussy was sore as shit.

I woke up the day after, with countless texts on my phone, ranging from Jesse threatening me, to Mia wondering where I was and what happened. I've been spending most of that time, productively looking her up. Going through all the details about her life through the diary Maisy so graciously gave me, and I've finally come to a conclusion.

This Fran is the same Fran that's been scribbled frantically in black ink over page thirty-eight. This Fran is the same Fran that tortured her daily. So, *this* Fran will be, you guessed it, the *same* Fran that I will take care of. I watch as she denies her friends offer for a ride back home.

What's wrong with this girl? Doesn't she know there's a serial killer out there? I'm different, I don't give a shit if death finds me. What I do care about, is if it finds me before I've finished my revenge. Nobody is out here late at night. Lincoln State Park is a fifteen-minute walk from where she lives, so I decided to spend the day staying as close to her and her friends as I could.

The three of them are oblivious. Who knew Fran was the outdoorsy type. I chuckle to myself. They jump in the car, and she waves them off. With earbuds playing music, she obliviously passes me in the treeline. I need to make my move now. If I don't, I might not get another chance.

Walking behind her, I check my surroundings to make sure nobody else is about. It's late, who the fuck would be. Lifting my arm, I strike. Once, because I don't want to kill her, just knock her out. The minute her skull connects with the rock in my hand she falls to the floor like a sack of fucking shit, and I finally release that breath that was, coincidentally, stuck in my throat.

Even if someone saw me now, they wouldn't know who I was. I'm wearing a balaclava with some fucking skull mask design over the top. Nothing but my bright blue eyes on show. Taking her by the wrists, I drag her down into the brush and over the ditch.

Deeper into the treeline and far away from the road as I can. If this was a year ago, I'd never have been able to drag a limp body like this. Dead weight is so fucking hard. However now, I do this with ease. *I think.*

Who am I kidding this shit is fucking hard. This is why there's hardly *any* female serial killers and also why we act mostly in crimes of passion. The workload is too much and dragging around bodies isn't something we are interested in doing. Shit, I wouldn't be dragging poor Fran through the woods if it wasn't absolutely necessary. Not that I'm planning to continue this after I've killed everyone. Let's think of this as more of a means to a beautiful end.

My goal here is to hurt everyone who hurt Maisy and unfortunately, Fran will feel the brunt of it. This is my first time after all, and I have absolutely no idea what I'm doing. But I've watched enough crime shows to get the gist.

"Come on, wake up." I slap Fran's cold little cheek three more times. She's been out for the past thirty minutes. It's laughable really. Who would've thought a rock would do that much damage.

"Fran," I sing. Her eyes shoot open and instantly she's frantic, tearing at the rope I've tied to her wrists above her head. I may have also managed to hoist her over one particularly strong looking tree branch.

"Wha-what's going on?" She asks, her lips quiver in fear. Frantically looking around at her surroundings as the panic builds in her eyes and I'm so fucking turned on by it. She panics, her eyes darting from left to right. "Help!!" she screams.

The sound piercing through my ears the same way it does when a child has that awful high pitched fucking scream as they cry. God, I hate kids.

"Help!!!" she screams again.

"Fran… Fran!" I hold my hands up. "Nobody will be able to hear you. We're out in the middle of nowhere. And even if they did, they'll never make it in time." My voice coming out slightly muffled due to the balaclava. In that moment, the realisation hits her, and she begins to sob.

"Please, I have so much to do." Tears streaming from her eyes.

"What, like sucking more dick," I chortle. "Don't make me laugh Fran, your fucking life is worthless," I sigh. "I'm not getting into an argument with you. I came here to ask you a few questions."

"Whatever you want, I-I'll give it to you," she stutters.

"Oh, I know you will." I pull the knife from the back of my jeans waistband.

She begins to scream even louder this time and if she carries on, I'll cut the tongue from her mouth. Shaking the knife in front of her, I continue. "First thing, I hate repeating myself. So, when I speak, listen, and listen well. Get it?" Fran nods. "Good." I smile behind the mask. "Now. Tell me about Maisy Lee."

"Who?"

"What did I just say about repeating myself. Also, don't lie to me either," I chuckle now. "OH!" I shout and she flinches. "I forgot to say that each lie you tell me; I'll make a small cut to that pretty little face. Small enough to be quick but deep enough to scar you bad. So, one last chance. Maisy Lee, talk."

She sobs. Still struggling in those restraints. It's pathetic really. "HELP ME!"

"HELP ME!! HELP ME!!" I repeat. Turning round and round in circles, screaming into the cold night air and the sight of her flinching back in fear makes me wild.

"Nobody's going to hear you." I burst out laughing, unable to hold it in anymore.

"So, stop. Fucking. Crying." I bring the knife to her face, gripping her chin with my free hand as I press the tip of the blade just under her right eye. "I will pop your fucking eyeball out. Speak!" I scream the final word in her face.

"M-Maisy Lee, was m-my roommate."

"And?" I press.

"S-she k-killed herself last year."

"And why did she kill herself, Fran?" I step back. "Riddle me that."

"I don't-"

"Liar!!" I shout again. My hand connects with her cheek, and she spins in a circle.

Desperately trying to keep her balance on her tiptoes. I grind my teeth together, grabbing her by the hips and turning her back to face me.

"Fran, I promise you if the next words out of your mouth aren't the truth, I'm going to lose my mind."

"S-she killed herself because-" She closes her eyes. "Because we bullied-"

"Because you bullied her enough for her to think her life was worthless!" I finish the sentence for her considering she's too chicken shit to do it herself. As I close the space between us and press the blade into the skin on her cheek a guttural sound rings out.

Blood seeping out as I press harder, and deeper. Slicing through the skin like butter. Her screams and blubbering fill the air around me. Her breath turning white from the freezing cold night air.

"Please," she cries again, blood pouring from her face. "I-I d-didn't."

"You didn't what?" I cut her off. I'm losing my fucking patience with this girl. "You didn't mean to?"

I laugh, spinning in a circle. Jesus, if I saw me right now, even I'd think I was crazy. "Don't worry though, it wasn't just you." Fran is hysterical now. Snot dripping from her perfect little button nose. "I know exactly who helped you," I chuckle.

"Sarah Chambers and Elena Michaels. They'll meet the same fate soon enough. I watched you guys earlier in fact."

"Please," she begs again.

"Please? Did you stop when she begged?" I press. "When she was laying on the shower floor crying after you beat her for the third time that day, as your friends watched, laughing as she sobbed."

"I'm sorry."

"No you're not." I roll my eyes.

"Please!" She cries. Her begging is becoming increasingly more frustrating.

"It's too late for that." I cut her face again and I don't stop until she's a bloody mess. I watch as she chokes on her own screams and the tears seep into the sliced skin.

"This is her revenge. *This* is what she wanted. You pushed her. Day in and day out. Made her feel like she was *nothing* when she was the most beautiful thing in this disgusting world." Tears begin to well in my eyes, but I wipe them away with the back of my hand. Grabbing Fran by the throat. "When she was my fucking angel!" I shriek.

"Wait," her words a blubbering mess, "please I can tell you w-who-"

I begin laughing hysterically. "You think I don't know all of it? I know what you and your friends did to her. I know what *he* did to her. And I'll make sure everyone else does."

"W-what?"

"The day you started; was the day I slowly lost the love of my life. The one person who saw *me* and loved ME!" I get in her face, bellowing the last word. Her sobs and coughing wrack her tiny little frame. Her voice raw. I'm probably no better than the killer that's out there right now.

"I'm s-sorry… P-please." Her begging, gross, it's making me feel sick.

"The begging is becoming pathetic now, Fran. Really, very tedious."

"I can-"

She tries to continue talking but I cut her off again.

"Maisy was the only part of me that was good. The single most precious thing in my life and you," my voice cracks, the burn at the back of my throat runs up to my nose. "You took her from me. So now I'm taking something from the ones that love you. Now, I'm going to ruin their life like you ruined mine."

A twig snaps behind me and I freeze, pivoting on my heel ever so slowly as my eyes rake over the figure dressed head to toe in black.

"Well, well, well," he claps. "Look who's more like me than I initially thought." He rolls his arm in a circle in front of him and takes a bow.

"Casanova?" I breathe. I don't really know if it's him, his face is covered.

"God, I fucking hate that shit," he groans, taking a few steps forward.

"So, what should I call you?" What the fuck am I doing engaging with him? This is the guy who's been killing women everywhere and I'm just, what, engaging in conversation with a serial killer. Maisy's death really did fuck me up, huh? He takes another step forward and I aim the knife at him.

"Uh, uh." I shake my head from side to side. "Don't."

He holds his hands up in surrender, stopping immediately. "Ok," he says. "You can call me The Shadow, I guess."

"Bit shit, really," I shrug, screwing my face up in disgust.

"You think?"

"It doesn't matter what I think," I shrug again. "Are you planning to kill me?"

"At some point, yes. But right now, I'm really enjoying this if I'm honest." His deep American accent is one I can't seem to place.

His black eyes stare into me from a distance and I'm honestly transfixed by them.

"Do I get to kill her first?" I nod my head back slightly towards Fran.

"Do you... What?" He looks at me, shock at my statement lacing his face. Fran continues to sob and scream for help behind me.

I groan at the sound because I genuinely can't believe that: A, I'm standing toe to toe with a fucking serial killer; and B, that I'm actually about to kill Fran. He barks out a laugh and claps.

"You, my love, can do anything you want to right now, as long as I get to watch." I tip my head to the side. Do I need to mull this over at all? I mean, he's here right now and either way I'm dead, so I may as well get one kill off before I am.

"Fine by me," I shrug. Turning back to face, Fran. I look at her as she hangs there perfectly still, watching the exchange between us, clearly confused. I'm really taking a chance turning my back to a serial killer, but I guess if I die now, at least I'm taking one of them with me.

"Sorry, Fran but I guess our time together has been cut short." I remove the mask from my face and her eyes widen in shock, I brush a few stray strands of hair from my face and smile.

"Ashley?" My name comes out as little more than a whisper.

"What does it feel like, knowing I'm the last thing you'll ever see?" Tilting my head, my smile now a crazy grin.

"No, no, no wait please-" I cut her pleading off with the first piercing of the knife in her chest. She freezes, looking into my eyes.

The knife is lodged in there pretty deep, and I struggle at first to pull the knife out. I see a leather gloved hand in my peripheral and yank one more time. Removing it from her chest plate. Laughing as the blood spurts everywhere, hitting my face, hands, and chest.

The serrated edge of the hunting knife piercing Fran's skin as I rain down blows to her chest, has me smiling from ear to ear.

"This is for every time you broke her!" I scream. Pounding into her chest the same way a hammer hits a nail. The sounds of her screams mingled with my heavy panting as I continue to destroy her body.

She deserves it, she deserves every ounce of pain that this fucking knife, that I, am giving her. I hope in her final moments, she's using what's left of that pathetic brain to think about all the awful things she's done.

About all the time she wasted being a vomit inducing, disgusting human being. I hope that when she takes her final breath on this earth, Maisy pops into her mind. I've never been happier knowing that the last emotion Fran felt, was fear.

Because she deserved it. She deserved it all. Each time the hunting knife pierces her skin, her screams of pain become less and less until the only sound is that of my panting and crying.

Why the fuck am I crying?

I'm holding onto the knife that's still lodged into her sternum. Her head now limp, and her chest is covered in knife marks, blood pouring from each wound. Turning her once white jeans crimson. A hand encases my wrist and I snatch it back, but his grip is too harsh.

"Get off me!"

"You're fucking perfect, Ashley," he whispers, pulling me close to him as he sniffs my hair.

In a split second he pushes me back, letting go of me, and I stumble. I watch as he takes small, calculated steps towards me and I mimic him until my back hits the tree trunk behind me.

"Look at you, releasing all that pent up aggression. Why?"

"Weren't you listening?" I hiss.

Why the fuck am I not scared? What's fucking wrong with me?

Leaning into my neck, he begins to smell me. His mask running over my cheek and the nylon fabric tickling my jawline. I should be running right now, running for my life, but where am I going to go. My car is parked a little ways from here and who's to say he won't get me before I reach it.

"So beautiful. Covered in someone else's blood," he breathes in my ear, the tone bringing a shiver to my body I've never experienced before. "So perfect." I turn my face to look at him, to show him I'm not afraid and to defy what he wants me to be.

"I'm not afraid," I whisper. "I'm not afraid to die, just not yet. Please let me finish what I started."

"Oh, I'm not going to kill you right now, my girl."

My girl?

"Then what?" I press. He brings his gloved hand up to the bottom of his mask, peeling the black fabric from his face and folding it up to his nose. Just enough that his mouth is on show. A slow but beautiful smile creeps over his face and the pooling between my legs is evident.

Do I like this? No. Wait, do I?

He pokes his tongue out, then proceeds to flatten it against my cheek. Licking the remnants of Fran's life force off me. "I'm going to fuck you against this tree, and you're going to love every single second."

The pop of the button on my jeans causes me to flinch and I close my eyes. An involuntarily moan releasing as he rips the zip down and yanks the jeans roughly down my thighs.

"Don't," I beg, but I don't mean it, and by the way he laughs so sweetly in my ear, he knows it too. Grabbing my shoulders, he spins me on the spot.

"Are you wet for me?"

"No." Another laugh. He runs his hand over my face, spreading the blood onto his glove as he reaches between my legs and begins to use it as lube against my swollen clit. My head drops back and hits his shoulder at the invasion of his touch against my skin.

I hear the zip from his own jeans fall and in a split second, without any warning, he thrusts inside me like a man possessed. The tree bark grinds against my blood-soaked cheek.

"Fuuuck!" He cries out. Leaning forward, he licks the blood from my cheek again. It's vile and depraved. So why the fuck do I feel the butterflies in my lower stomach? "That's my sick and twisted little angel." The words are guttural and raw in my ear as he continues to rub my clit with every single thrust.

"Oh my god," I breathe out. All the while feeling the fullness of his fat cock thrusting in and out of me. He thrusts in harder, branding my slick walls.

He's not even wearing a condom. I'm just letting him fuck me raw like it's nothing. Like it's normal. He slides his other hand round my throat and pulls me against him, my back stretched into the most awkward but deliciously curved angle as the tip of his cock rubs against that perfect little sweet spot.

"Harder." The words leave my mouth before I can stop them and with that, he begins to fuck me so roughly that I forget how to breathe. "Fuck me harder!"

Have I lost my damn mind? Definitely.

"You want harder?" he roars, immediately pulling himself out of me. Fisting my hair he drags me over to Fran's weightless body, still hanging from the tree.

He throws me to the ground as the broken twigs and dirt bite into my bare knees.

"On your back, Ashley." Flipping me over with a black booted foot and proceeding to press it to my chest. Holding me in place.

"What the fuck are you doing?!" I shout, pressing my hands into the sole of his boot, to relieve some of the pressure from my chest.

"Giving you what you want!" he growls down at me. Removing a knife from his thigh, he rips open Fran's shirt and slices her stomach open. Her blood cascades over me as I reach up and cover my face just in time, before her entrails fall from her gut.

Dropping to the floor he flips me over, bracing me on all fours as he forces his way back inside me. I'm absolutely covered in blood. *Her* blood as he fucks me.

Grabbing my upper arms in a vice like grip he drags me back against his chest. He is on his knees behind me as my jeans tied legs are between his. I don't realise I'm moaning until a harsh scream ruptures from my throat.

"That's it. Look at her," he sings. "Look at what you did to her while I fuck this tight little cunt." His voice ringing in my ears as he talks to me. My orgasm building with every single thrust. "Widen your legs for me," he begs. "I need to touch you."

I involuntarily widen my knees as I see him bite the leather of his glove.

Tearing it from his hand, running it over the blood covered fabric, he uses it to coat my swollen and extremely angry clit yet again, rubbing back and forth.

"Yes, oh fuck, yes," I cry out. I open my eyes and stare up at Fran hanging there as her body rocks back and forth ever so slightly, the cold breeze washing over me as he fucks me from behind. Our skin slapping and echoing into the night.

Hearing the deep rumble in his chest as he shoots his load inside me, makes me jump over the edge with him and it's fucking incredible. The orgasm waves over my skin and sends shivers through every single pore. Our heavy breathing the only sound within the forest and he drops his forehead against my back.

"That's a first," he begins laughing. He immediately pulls out of me, and I turn to face him, dragging my jeans back up the best I can.

"Get out of here. I'll take care of this."

What?

I freeze in place as he rights himself. Not looking at me. "I don't-"

He looks at me then, raising his arm and shouting, pointing which way for me to go. "Go Ashley!"

I flinch, pulling up my jeans up further as I walk backwards.

"Get the fuck out of here."

I flick my eyes to Fran's lifeless body, my knife still lodged inside her, before I bolt out of there.

ASHLEY

Waking up the day after murdering Fran in the woods surprised me. But not as much as the realisation that the person responsible for killing all the women within a two-mile radius, is the man I just allowed to fuck me. So, let me get this straight. In the space of a few weeks, I've had three cocks inside me.

Hmm. Funny how things work out.

I thought I would wake up feeling some type of way. Like, I don't know… sick or something. Like I'd been violated by someone who cuts women's hearts out. Yet, all I feel is calm. Having sex with a serial killer, wasn't exactly how I saw the night ending, but what can you do?

At least it was good.

My heart feels like it's about to explode. I got revenge for Maisy last night and the pleasure I felt waking up this morning, had no comparison to anything else in my life. I felt nothing about what I did.

I didn't feel anything when I showered and got dressed this morning. I didn't feel anything when I strolled into Psych 101 over fifteen minutes late. And I don't feel anything now as I open up my locker to put my books away before I head to the cafeteria for lunch.

All I'm able to think about is the fact that he helped me get rid of the body. Made sure I was away from the scene. I haven't been able to stop thinking about the man in black since I got into bed last night.

Closing up my locker, I turn around only to be met with the faces of two people I'm really not interested in engaging with right now. Mainly because I'm not ready for them to die yet.

I move to the left and both of them block me. Jesus, I know where this is going. So, I move to the right, and they repeat the action. Sighing, I roll my eyes and look directly at Jesse. The bruise that runs from the bridge of his nose and underneath both eyes, makes me smirk.

"Nice welt, sweetie," I chuckle. Immediately, he pushes me back against the lockers and the metallic sound echoes down the hallway. "Not necessary. But I'll bite."

"You broke my fucking nose." Yeah, he's really angry.

"And you raped to me. Blah, blah, blah." I circle my hand between us, hoping that this ridiculous conversation goes quicker than I expect but I highly doubt it. "We could continue this conversation all day and neither of us would get anywhere."

"I didn't give you anything you didn't want."

"Because I really asked to be fucked by you." This guy really is nuts. I might have killed his ex-girlfriend last night but this motherfucker's an out and out rapist. He steps forward, getting closer in my face to the point that I can taste last night's alcohol on his breath.

"Do some drinking last night, huh?" A hand wraps around my throat and tightens. "Marcus," I choke out. "Finally got the balls to drop after I kicked them into your throat?" I laugh with what's left of the air in my lungs. Mainly because I know these assholes won't kill me in the hallway. They don't have the balls.

He squeezes tighter and I smile, black spots dancing around my eyes. Little do they both know I love this fucking shit.

Choke me harder, daddy.

I turn my head to face Marcus and try my best to give him the cutest smile I can.

"Harder. I... like... that," I breathe with every single word. Pulling me forward and then smashing me back against the lockers, the metal clangs, as the back of my head connects with them. Jesse grabs my jaw, angling it in his direction.

"If you open your fucking mouth about what happened, I'll fuck that tight little ass of yours till you bleed. With or without your fucking consent."

"Wouldn't be the first time." Even though I have little to no oxygen reaching my brain right now, even though my lungs are burning as they're starved for air, I won't let him think I'm afraid. I won't allow him the satisfaction from me like he did the night he raped Maisy.

The night she tried to call me, but I was too busy at the cinema with a friend. The night I became her last hope. When everything was said and done, I'd beg for her forgiveness for the rest of my life if I have to. I'll never allow myself a single moment of happiness ever again. She needed me and I was too busy. I wasn't there.

"I'll kill you, Ashley," Marcus presses his nose to my face as he releases the words in what he thinks is a threat.

Nothing like that scares me. I'm waiting for death. I can feel my face going red, the veins in my forehead protruding to the surface. Jesse taps his hand, and he releases me. I desperately suck in heavy breaths and drop my head back against the lockers, coughing.

My eyes darting between the both of them. I haven't said anything about Jesse's little stunt the other night and in all honesty, I never planned to.

I wanted him to sweat. Be afraid that I could ruin him. Instead, he's choosing to make this as though I wanted it, like I deserved it. I only intended to piss Fran off, to have her walk into the bathroom and see him on his knees eating my pussy or my ass, whichever came first really.

I never asked to be fucked. Nobody asks to be raped. A bubble of laughter balls up in my lower stomach as the air seeps into my lungs and I take those much needed, calming breaths.

"What's so fucking funny?" Jesse seethes, his face screwed up like someone killed his dog.

"You think threatening to kill me is going to scare me?"

"It should do Ashley; I don't make empty threats," he snarls. I stand up straighter and take a step towards him. My face blank, looking up at him through my eyebrows, giving my best Kubrick stare.

"Well, it doesn't. And you know why?" I wait for an answer, but it never comes. "Because I'll climb in the window of your fucking frat house, walk up the stairs and cut your fucking throat in your sleep. I know what you did to that girl last year."

The moment the words leave my lips, the realisation hits him, and his features begin to soften. Fear marring his face as Maisy's name probably flitters through his memory like a stain he can't remove.

"I know everything." From the corner of my eye, I see Marcus' mouth drop open slightly as he looks towards his brother. The feeling of watching him squirm is way too enjoyable as the corner of my mouth curves up into an odious smirk.

"What's going on here?" I know that voice. Within a split second I mask my face with a beautiful smile and turn to face Nathan.

"Nothing, Professor Danvers. Jesse and Marcus were just asking to help carry my things to the cafeteria." Turning back to face them I smile harder, baring my teeth. "Right boys?" I wink in their direction.

"She hurt herself at the frat party the other day, so we just wanted to make sure she was ok." Jesse lies. The muscles in his jaw rippling through his skin as he grinds his teeth together.

"Always helpful to new starters," Marcus jumps in, a fake grin curling his mouth.

"Miss Porter, join me in my office. I have to discuss matters of the pop quiz with you." Nathan places both his hands in the pockets of his navy slacks and nods his head to the left, gesturing for me to gather my things and follow him. I stare deep into Jesse's soul as I reply.

"Sure thing." Bending down, I pick up my backpack, leaning into his ear as I stand. "Sleep well fucker. Make sure your doors and windows are locked." I shoulder check him on my way past and fall in step with Nathan as I follow him back to his office. No doubt for a little têt-á-têt.

127

"Thanks for that," I whisper.

"Everything ok?" he asks, looking down at me briefly as we make our way down the hallway.

"Nothing I can't handle myself, that's for sure." I thread one arm through both straps on the backpack, lifting it up onto one shoulder.

"We'll talk about it later." he breathes through his nose. His face is usually without an ounce of expression, however right now, he seems to be infuriated.

"We won't." I roll my eyes, punching in a text to Mia that I won't be able to meet her and the team for lunch as something came up. As he pushes me through the front door of the receptionist's office, I screw my face up at her. I've seen her in the hallways here and there and for some reason she's taken a major disliking to me.

I'm about done here already, and I'm also in no mood to have anyone being happy around me. I know what he's calling me in here for and I wonder whether this is what he was like before me. The receptionist looks at me in disgust and I begin laughing.

Ashley, please. Remember our plan.
Remember what we decided to do.

I'm hearing Maisy more and more lately. The closer I get to avenging her death, the more she enters my mind and I find solace within the sound of her beautiful voice. Living on this earth without her for the past year has given me nothing but sadness and a desire to hurt all those who hurt her.

Fran was always going to be first. She started this, and set in motion the pain that Maisy was enduring every day during her first year at Brown. Next on my list are those fucking rats she calls her friends.

I have the perfect plan for them and I'm so excited about it I can't wait. Quick and easy. Knowing that soon enough, I'll be hearing their screams as I watch them slowly die, is turning me on.

Yeah, I think I might be a little more messed up that I initially thought.

"Sit." Pushing me into the leather chair in front of his desk, he turns the lock on the door, moving to sit on the edge of his desk, right in front of me. In all his glory looking like a fucking GQ model and with the way I feel now, having him fuck me in the ass might actually calm me down. Stop my brain from overthinking and I might be able to get some fucking peace from my inner thoughts. Leaning back in the seat, I roll my lips together and look up at him.

"So, what was that?" He presses.

"Nothing." Curling my fingers into my palm, looking at my nails. Uninterested in what he has to say. When I got back to the dorms last night, thankfully everyone was asleep in their rooms. The car I used to take the late-night drive back to school was a rental. I cleaned as much of the blood from my body, and the car as I could, making sure nothing could be traced back to me.

I stripped all my clothes off in the shower and cleaned every single inch of my body and the ceramic tiles on the walls. I made perfectly sure that there was no evidence available for anyone to find.

"It didn't look like nothing, Ashley," Nathan says, pulling me from my thoughts.

"I'd rather not talk about it, if it's all the same. I'd prefer to have you buried in my pussy." Looking up to the ceiling he closes his eyes. I hate that sex with him is the only thing I've *felt* in a long time. Resting my hands on the arms of the chair I push myself to stand. Sliding my hands between his legs, I take a step forward.

"Ashley," he murmurs the moment I reach for the button of his navy suit trousers.

"You don't want me?" Softening my eyes as I give him that doe eyed look that he loves so much. Taking hold of his hand in both of mine, I slide it slowly down between my breasts. His eyes following every single inch until he meets the waistband of my shorts.

"What happened to your knees?" The crease between his eyebrows becoming deeper as he looks down.

"I tripped during cheer practice," I shrug, hopefully he believes me. I don't really think explaining to him that I stabbed the woman he was fucking last year is a good idea really. I suck my bottom lip between my teeth and bite down. Looking up at him, he mirrors me and looks into my eyes. I know he wants me by the pained expression on his face.

"Why do I feel like that's a load of shit?" He holds my chin between his thumb and forefinger. "What really happened? Let me help you."

Help me?

Yeah right.

It's impossible for anyone to help me now. I've taken the longest stride over a line that I can never come back from, and I don't want help. I want everything but that. I want to punish those who deserve it.

"Touch me… Please," I beg.

I've come to crave his touch more and more as the days go on and today it's even worse. After last night, and the way that sicko had his hands all over my body, the way my pussy aches to be touched by him again… is sickening.

I need Nathan to replace this feeling with his own. I need him to remove every single fingerprint that the sick bastard left on me. I mean, not that I'm any better. I'm just as sick really.

"You're killing me, love."

"Just a little bit. I need you, Nathan, please."

"Jesus Christ. Can this wait?" He looks at me, placing his hands on my shoulders. "Someone could hear."

I take a step closer, lacing both my hands on either side of his face and bringing him in for a gentle peck on the lips.

"I'll be quiet, I promise," I mewl. "Make me come all over this desk, I need you so bad." Last time I was in this assholes office I blacked out.

The only way I knew he finished off inside me was after I woke up on his leather couch with his cum dripping out of me.

"Please," I whine. He stands up and I take a single step back, he grabs my waist spinning me and pulls my back flush to his chest. His hand rises to my chin as he turns my face to meet his.

Our lips millimetres apart and the anticipation of his kiss is driving me insane. I don't know what's gotten into me since I started fucking him. I knew offering him anal would be the deciding factor.

"Ask me again," he growls.

"Put your fingers inside me," I mewl against his mouth, the gentle breath from my words hitting his lips as he leans in and kisses me deeply.

Devouring me with a single kiss all while working my cycling shorts past my hips and over my ass. They pool at my feet, and I step out of them as he slides himself further back onto the desk, taking me with him. We don't usually kiss like this.

Today though, I can't get enough. We're all teeth and tongues as we fight for who has control over the kiss. He wraps his left arm under my chin, pulling my head back against his shoulder. As he glides his hand up and over my mouth, leaving my nose free so I can breathe.

"Put one foot on either side of my legs, spread yourself open for me." I follow his instructions putting myself on full display for him.

I'm absolutely drenched with the anticipation of having him touch me, having his fingers inside me.

"I'm going to need you to be quieter than you have ever been, Ashley. This is not a joke. Do you understand what I'm telling you?"

"Yes, I understand." My words come muffled from behind his hand but I'm pretty sure he gets the idea. With my heart thumping behind my chest, I lift my head and watch as he presses two fingers inside me.

"Soaking for me as always, love." Within a split second, he inches inside me, as his girth fills me, stretching me in sheer pleasure.

ASHLEY

It's been five days and Fran's body still hasn't turned up. The whole school is going crazy. Her parents and so-called friends have been frequently on the news begging her to either come back home, or for whoever has her to please let her go. Well, only I, and one other person know Fran's not coming back.

Ever.

I have absolutely no idea where he's buried her, or even if she's going to be found at all. He could've chopped her up into tiny pieces by now and I'd never know. I might be the only person in this school man enough to say I really don't give a fuck about Fran.

I mean, I killed her after all. But everyone else is acting like she wasn't the biggest fucking bitch to ever walk the halls of Brown University. Although watching her mother cry on TV hasn't brought me as much joy as I initially thought it would. Jesse and his stupid brother haven't been near me since the news broke that Fran had gone missing the evening of my first altercation with them.

Giving me time to watch my next victim without being interrupted. I decided to put Fran's little butt buddies to the back of the line for the meantime. I don't need to attract any unwanted attention. So here I am, standing outside the Dean's house. I decided that tonight was the night for him to meet his untimely demise.

Raising my hand, I rap my knuckles against the glass panelling. Making sure to keep my head down so nobody gets a good look at my face. Footsteps become louder the closer they get to the door. I look up and smile as Joseph pulls the door open.

"Miss Porter, what are you-"

"I'm so sorry, I got the address from Professor Danvers. My car broke down and I was wondering if I could use your phone to call breakdown?"

"Oh, uh, of course. Please," he steps back, opening the door and gesturing for me to enter. "Go through to the back room and take a seat."

"Thank you so much." I smile, stepping over the threshold of his house. I pull off my black heels and tug at the belt around my coat. Can't run in heels. Not that I need to but just in case. I slide the mack off my shoulders as the door clocks shut and turn to face him.

I came prepared tonight and pulled out the big guns. A blood red, velvet dress hugs my body, clinging in all the right places. It's freezing outside but who gives a fuck when what I'm about to do to him will warm me up.

I have to be quick though, I need to make my way to a study group Nathan set up for the three students who are falling behind in his class. He asked me to attend this evening and seeing as I had nothing else to do -other than this- I agreed to help. I have exactly one hour to get this done, change and leave without anyone seeing me.

Talk about cutting it short.
This needs to be quick and easy.
No mess.

Walking into the back room, I take a seat on the sofa and place my clutch bag on the seat next to me. The fat fuck walks into the room and for a moment he freezes on the spot at the sight of me. Let's play it safe here.

"Just coming back from a date," I laugh dryly. "Needless to say, it did *not* go well." I giggle, brushing my hands down my dress as though I'm nervous.

"Boys these days wouldn't know how to treat a young woman such as yourself even if it was right in front of them."

"Do you?" I tilt my head.

"Do I what, Miss Porter?" Resting his hand on the arm of the chair he drops down into the seat. His rotund belly wiggling as he does, and I have to do everything not to grimace. I can't believe I'm about to do this. The thing in front of me is nearly seventy, with type two diabetes and more liver spots on his hands and face than I've ever seen.

He's balding on top and doing everything he can to cover the patch with what's left of his hair. If the liver spots weren't going to give me the ick, the combover certainly has. Swallowing down the bile, I smile.

"Know how to treat a woman," I shrug, looking nonchalantly around the room. Joseph clears his throat as he shuffles in his seat. God, he's vile. "This big house. All alone. Is there no wife in the picture?"

"She died, a while ago now. So, no. I'm a lonely man in this house." I lean forward, knowing full well that my breasts are on display. Joseph's eyes linger on my body as I stand. I stalk over like a cat and the poor bastard has no idea what's about to happen. He doesn't take his eyes off of me for a single second.

"Can I use your phone to call triple A?" Lifting his finger, he points to the phone next to the fireplace and I smile. "Thank you." I turn and make my way to the table, picking up the receiver and holding it to my ear.

"Would you like a drink while you wait?"

Bingo.

"If you give me a moment to sort this, I'll make it for us." My seductive tone sings through the air as I look over my shoulder at him and wink. The fucker's dick is already growing, and this is the dirtiest I've ever felt. And not in a good way either. Pressing a few random buttons, I put on the best performance of my life.

"Yes, hi. I was wondering if I could have someone come out to collect me and my car." I laugh. "Yeah, I broke down on Winchester Road... uh huh... yes that's right, just past the park. Thank you. Ok... yes, I'm safe. Ok, bye." I put down the phone, taking a deep breath. I need to steady my nerves. He might be fat, but he's bigger and most likely stronger than me. I need to be careful and make sure it counts. "Where are the drinks?"

He points to the corner at the back of the room, and I make my way over. Pouring the whiskey into a tumbler, I carefully lift the vile of crushed Temazepam from between my cleavage and pour it into the glass. Not that he will be able to taste the difference.

I check my watch as I rest my arms on the back of the sofa. I've watched him talk absolute shit for what feels like fucking ages. The Temazepam has finally started to kick in and it's the first time I've thanked God for anything. His words are becoming slurry, but he's fighting it. There were enough crushed tablets in there to put down a fucking horse and with his diabetes and lack of taste, it was easy to get him to drink.

"How long will the recovery team take to get here?" He slurs slightly.

"Another five minutes, I'd say." I look him up and down. "Do you think I'm sexy?"

"Ashley, I don't-" He's taken to calling me by my first name now. He's had three drinks in thirty minutes so the effects of the alcohol would mask the sleeping tablets for him.

"Oh, come on. I've seen the way you look at me, Mr Chambers," I interrupt, I don't want to give him a chance to steer away from the conversation. I stand up, curve my fingers around the hem of my velvet dress and pull it up and over my head. Standing in front of him in nothing but a matching set of pink underwear. His eyes widen as he looks me over, taking in every single inch of my body.

"Beautiful," he breathes out. The tip of his tongue darting over his lips, swiping left to right and coating them with thick saliva. I'm going to definitely need to be fucked after this. This man is gross. "Come here," he curves his finger and I walk towards him. "Take off your bra," he breathes, his erection growing.

But not that much. I reach behind my back, unclasping the hooks of the bra and let it drop to the floor, displaying my breasts for him. My nipples peaking instantly from the warmth in the room. Kneeling between his legs, I run my hands up his thighs and grip the buckle of his belt.

"I was thinking, I should thank you for helping me tonight." I unbuckle the belt. "It can be our little secret?"

He huffs out a laugh, tossing back the rest of the whiskey in his glass. Dropping his head back onto the seat. "Make it good, Ashley," he sighs. "Choke on it for me."

I'm going to need to scrub my body later.

"Keep your eyes closed for me," I purr. "Let me take care of you."

He shuffles in his seat as I pull the zip of his trousers down to reveal his tighty-whities. Wrapping my hand around his tiny little dick I grimace. That's it, it's official, I'm cutting this fucking hand off later, his groans fill the room as I begin to slide my hand up and down his shaft. He simply sits there, mouth open and a grin displayed for the world to see.

This man couldn't be happier about the aspect of a nineteen-year-old girl deepthroating his mummified penis. I might be fucking a man who is thirty-eight, but at least he looks like a Greek god. At least he fucks me in such a depraved way that I beg for more. Shit, I've even been fucked by the local serial killer and even *this* is worse than *that*.

Reaching around the back of my knickers, I wrap my fingers around the syringe, keeping my eyes on him, but he's far too busy enjoying this to notice. I bite the cap off the end and gently, *very gently,* pierce the skin, squeezing the contents inside him. Pulling away, I lean back on my knees and stand up. Snatching my bra from the floor, I put it back on and make my way back over to the sofa. Lifting my previously discarded dress from the arm of the chair, I slide it back on.

"What are you doing?!" Joseph demands. "Get back here and suck me off!"

Well that kicked in quicker than I thought.

"Jesus, you could be a little more polite about it considering you're about to have a fucking heart attack." I turn around, sitting back on the couch in front of him and smiling. "You have enough Temazepam in your system to put out a horse and enough Fentanyl to kill one," I sigh, leaning back.

"What are you," He shakes his head, trying to clear the buzz, "talking about?"

"I drugged you," I grin.

Joseph begins to laugh. "I like role playing," he holds up his hands, laughing. "I'm so scared."

"You should be." I check my watch and smile. "It will start to kick in soon. I'd say," I look at him, "in about thirty seconds." Tucking my hair behind my ears, I stare at him. Waiting for it all to kick in. "Joseph, you already look like you're going to pass out from lack of sleep alone. I clearly didn't give you enough because you should've been unconscious way before now."

"This is some kind of joke, right?" His brows furrow as he stares into my eyes. Waiting for my laughter, I guess. But this is no laughing matter. This is really happening.

"I don't joke. Cross my heart it's real." Taking the proof from my purse, I lean in and show him. "See." His eyes flick to the syringe and then back to meet mine. His facial expressions aren't quite there yet but his eyes... It's all in the eyes. "I know you believe me now. Your eyes give you away."

"Why?" A simple word, with so many answers.

"That word holds so much weight, but I'll start simple for you. That way you can understand everything up until the point your heart gives out."

He blinks rapidly and shakes his head. "What the fu-" The sound of him coughing and clearing his throat makes me smile even wider. So wide my cheeks begin to burn.

I didn't expect to enjoy this as much as I do. Number two on my list. I never would've put myself down for a murderer though. I guess I just didn't have a reason until now.

"You remember Maisy Lee." He looks at me instantly, his face draining of colour as the realisation hits him.

"You're..."

"We're not talking about me, Joseph; we're talking about her now. So, keep up will you. She sadly ended her life last year. Why?" The look on his face proves that what I'm doing to him, is worth it. There's nothing. No realisation for him. He truly believes that what he did to her was normal.

"Do you even remember what *you* did to her?"

"I didn't do anything to her!" He snarls.

"Come on, I think we're past the point of lying now, aren't we?"

"Excuse me?"

I'm calm, I know what I'm doing, and I know no one can stop me. I've watched the walrus here for the past week. Keeping out of sight the entire time. I know that he lives alone, has no friends, nobody who checks on him and absolutely no one that gives a fuck if he lives or dies.

I also know that Nathan will be next in line to take the dean position from him, and having Joseph out of the picture, will put him there. I also know that having Nathan there will make things so much easier for me in the near future too. Soon, I'll be watching this man die slowly before my eyes.

I'll watch as the blood begins to reverse itself up his arm and the pain in his chest becomes too much for him to handle. I just wish she was here to see it. I wish I could take back all the pain this sick fucker caused her.

"Do you remember her coming to you? Begging for help? Do you remember how you took advantage of her, forcing her to her knees in exchange for being kept safe from her bullies?"

"I don't know what-" the words are cut off by a round of coughs. "W-what you're talking about." He speaks through the onslaught, pressing his hand to his chest.

"Let me refresh your memory." Even from where I'm sitting, I can see that his pupils are already blown out from the drugs. Small beads of sweat beginning to form at his hairline and chest.

I mean, the man is still sitting there with his cock out. Not that there's much of it but still, he should put it away. This shouldn't take too long. That way I can clean everything up, remove any trace of myself and still make it to the study group in time.

I'm filled with rage, I want to stab him to death, cut his obese little body up in to tiny pieces and leave him scattered around the house for when the police arrive.

However, I can't do that. I don't want to do that. Not really. I want to watch him suffer, to watch him deteriorate, just like he watched her. I want to watch the panic form on his face the same way he did hers every single time.

"She came to you for help, and what did you do?" I wait for his answer. Taking in a deep breath, I cross my leg over my knee, watching his face become redder by the second as he begins to claw at his chest.

"If you're starting to feel dizzy, that's the Fentanyl. Don't worry too much though it will be over soon." Sticking his fingers down his throat he vomits over the side of the leather chesterfield. The dark brown liquid from the whiskey splattering on the cream carpet. "There's no need to ruin the carpet. Also, being sick won't help," I pick the invisible lint from my dress.

"I injected it into your bloodstream, you can't vomit that up. So, if you could be quiet for a moment, we could have this talk."

"You're s-sick." he chokes out. His words hoarse and I can already hear the panicked tones latching on to every single word he manages to get out.

"You sexually assaulted her. Continuously. For eight months." He laughs then with what little energy he has left and my face drops.

"I didn't give her anything she didn't want."

"She wanted help and you saw that as an opportunity to touch her, fuck her and ruin her innocence. You may not have fucked her with the button mushroom you call a dick but forcing her to her knees is the same thing."

"It's no different than what-" The coughing takes over and he tries to stand up, wabbling on his feet I watch as he falls to the floor.

"What?" Cupping my hand to my ear, I lean forward slightly. "Sorry, can you repeat that, I didn't quite hear you." With sweat coating his face and dripping to the end of his nose. He rolls over onto his back and grasps his arm.

"Oh… my… Please… help me."

"Look at you." I stand from the couch, placing a leg either side of him as I crouch down and sit on his chest. His breathing is sporadic now.

"You'll never… get away… with this." The words tight in his throat, he doesn't even believe his own words.

"Oh, no?" Raising my eyebrows, I lean in, my forearms resting on my knees. "Tell that to Francesa Lopez, you wouldn't believe how easy she was to kill."

There it is.

His eyes widen in realisation that he's not about to make it out of this. That he will in fact die here. And I have front row seats to the performance of a lifetime. Watching ever so calmly as the Fentanyl takes effect and brings on the heart attack.

"The best thing about this, they'll never know. By the time you're found in three days, the opioid will be out of your system and on tox reports, they don't check for synthetics. This will just be a sad state of affairs. I can see it now," I hold my hands up in front of me. "Joseph Chambers, Dean of Admissions at

Brown University, dead of suspected heart attack." I sigh in happiness.

Leaning forward again, I watch as he struggles to breathe, the blood vessels in his eyes popping as the attack to his heart takes over.

"This was the least you deserved," I whisper. "Too bad you won't be here to see the rest." Joseph releases his last breath and stills underneath me. "I expected more." I screw up my face. "Just going to clean everything up and then I'll be out of your hair."

Pressing my hands to my knees, I push to stand and step over the dead body. Humming a happy tune, as I make my way into the kitchen in search of cleaning products.

THE SHADOW

Watching Ashley walk around the university like she didn't just kill two people in the space of a week is jarring. Since hiding that girl's body, Ashley's all I've been able to think about. So much so, that it's given me a constant migraine ever since.

I haven't been able to stop watching her. I'm there as she walks to class, when she takes her nightly run - which is fucking dangerous by the way- and I'm even there when she showers.

It's crazy. I've never been this obsessed with being everywhere someone is before. It's like, the harder I try to ignore her, the more my brain won't allow it. It's like I'm in a constant state of denial. I want her, but I don't want to kill her. As of this moment, I'm watching her walk out of a fucking restaurant with a guy.

She's on a fucking date and I can't stand it. I've had to patiently sit here while he's had his grubby little hands all over her perfect body. All over what belongs to me. The sex in the forest last week was fucking incredible and I haven't been able to get my mind off it since it happened.

The way her soaking wet pussy sucked in every single inch of my cock, the way her breathy moans sounded in the silence and darkness of the woods. The way her whimpers tortured me, having me second guess killing her. No woman has ever had this effect on me before, living or dead for that matter.

I can't work out what it is about Ashley that has basically halted my desire to kill. Take the last three days for example, I was watching this woman I met at a bar just outside of town and not once have I had the desire to cut her heart out. I wasn't even able to get hard as the thoughts flowed into my mind's eye.

It's like I don't want to kill her anymore, but more like I want to kill *for* her now. The way she so elegantly stabbed that brunette girl to death gave me the biggest and most painful hard on of my life, and I knew then that fucking her would end the night perfectly.

It was almost as good as our first time.

Almost.

Granted, she won't have any recollection of that so I can't really ask her to compare the two. The pressure building behind my black combats is killing me and I shake all thoughts of fucking Ashley into the back of my mind.

Pressing my back close to the brick wall down the dark alley, I watch as she stops at her car with Mr I Fuck Kids. Because let's face it, the guy looks like a fucking paedophile.

"Well, that was fun." She smiles, and I feel the anger burn my skin.

That smile belongs to me.

"It was."

I want to punch that smug fucking look off his face. My girl presses her palms to his chest the moment he leans in to kiss what belongs to me.

"I don't think that's a good idea, David." Giving him a tight smile, she steps back. The look of disgust on his face tells me everything I need to know about this guy.

"I just spent a hundred bucks on you. The least you can do is suck my dick, bitch." He grabs the back of her neck and forces her for a kiss.

It takes every ounce of control I have left in my body, to stop myself from marching over there and stabbing him to death. Ashley's movement is swift as I watch her kick him right between the legs. He falls to the ground like a sack of shit as she proceeds to spit on him.

"Fuck you!" she screams over her shoulder, opening her car door and speeding out of the carpark.

"Oh, Ashley you shouldn't have," I laugh as I leave the shadows of the alley and cross the road towards him.

What a wonderful gift.

David's groggy sounds fill the room. Raising his head, he grimaces as he looks around the darkened room with nothing, but a single light turned on above his head.

It takes him a moment to register the thick ropes wrapped around his torso. I watch as his head snaps from left to right, looking at the cable ties that wrap round his wrists and the wooden arm rest of the chair he sits on.

"What the fuck?" The words quiet enough that if I wasn't in the room, I wouldn't hear them. Yet here I am, sitting in the pitch-black corner of the warehouse I have him tied up in. This place has been abandoned for a while and nobody comes out here anyway. This is the usual place I hold my victims till the eventuality of their untimely death.

"Hello!" His hard voice bounces off the cold and cracked stone walls and I end up wondering if this is what he sounds like when he has sex.

What the fuck.

Shaking the thought from my mind I lean forward on the chair, sucking the cold night air into my lungs. The mouldy smell running through the decayed warehouse makes the hair on my arms stand on end.

"Hello?" He repeats, again, and I groan in response, and he whips his head around, twisting what little movement he has of his body. "Hello?... Who's there?"

"Please shut up. Your voice is annoying." Bracing my hands on my knees, I push to stand and take three steps into the light. I'm dressed head to toe in black, with my hood pulled up and a balaclava on. Nothing but my eyes on show.

"I'd never have put you for a whiney little bitch just by looking at you." Rubbing my eyes with the heels of my palms.

"Who are you?" his voice filled with fear. Just how I like them. "Whatever you think I've done-" Curious about what he thinks I think he's done; I take another step forward and drag my chair behind me. The screeching of the wood against the cement floor makes me cringe.

"What exactly do you think that I think you could have possibly done?" I sit in the chair, resting the black machete on both my knees. Grinning behind my black mask. Not that he can see.

"The girl," he swallows, his throat bobbing up and down. "She… she wanted to have sex. She said she did and I-"

"Wait a second," I hold up my hand, silencing him as the words run through my mind. "Did you rape someone?" I chuckle, my voice muffled as he stares into my cold dead eyes.

"N-no I-" he begins to stutter.

"Did she tell you to stop?" I interject, begging, praying for him to tell me 'yes.'

"Help!!!" He screams again.

"Help!!" I stand up, mimicking him. "Help! Help!"

Cupping my hands on either side my mouth, I scream louder. Till my throat burns. I look down at him, the stillness of his body. His lean muscles pressing through the rope as he struggles to break free.

"David, David, stop." My hands embrace the top of his shoulders, my fingers squeeze into the soft woollen fabric of his surprisingly soft sweatshirt. "Is this Cashmere?"

"What?" He's clearly never been in a situation quite like this before.

"I hate repeating myself, but seeing as you're in a predicament, I'll ask one more time. Is. This. Cashmere?" I pinch the wool and roll it between my fingers.

"Y-yes."

"Nice…So, the girl you were on a date with tonight. She belongs to me and-"

"Look I don't want her; you can have her." Does he really think I've tied him up over a woman? I have but that's beside the point. The main point I've come to realise, is that this is the first time in a week I've been excited to end someone's life. And funnily enough, it's a man.

First time for everything I guess.

Bending down, I wrap my hand around the handle of the machete, I strategically place by his side, removing it from the guard.

"It would seem that mommy and daddy never taught you not to touch things that don't belong to you." I steady myself beside him, his eyes never leaving mine.

"Please, wait a second I don't-"

Lifting the machete above my head, I swiftly bring it down and the blade slices through his left hand in one fell swoop.

His screams of pain fill the warehouse as his hand flops to the floor. Blood squirting from his wrist. Closing my eyes, I revel in the sound as it pierces my eardrums, flowing down the entire length of my body.

Coming too, I focus on the other hand and hack that one off too. The squeals coming from his throat remind me of a pig. High pitched. I circle in front of him, watching as he writhes around in agony, blood pooling beneath his feet. Snot, tears and sweat covering his face.

"It's nearly over, just breathe with me." Usually, all that crap over his face would make me feel sick. I mean even the women I've killed don't look this bad. "Last one big guy."

Raising the machete again, this time holding it in both hands I slice through the air, aiming the blade to the side of his neck. As the blade travels towards its destination, everything slows down. My brain engaging with the action as though I'm in slow motion.

I watch as his eyes widen, and in that moment, time stops. I watch as the blade cuts through the skin, the tendons snapping back from the muscle as the metal glides through his neck. Blood spraying everywhere when I pull the blade loose.

Sweat building over my entire body as I rain down blow after blow. When David's head eventually falls to the ground, I drop the machete to the floor and one of two things register to me as I frantically play with the button and zip on my trousers.

One, that was quite possibly the most aggressive and messy murder I've ever committed and two, I'm desperately stroking my cock at the sight of David's headless body in front of me.

I've never felt this turned on in my life. I've never wanted to please myself this way either.

"Holy fucking shit," I breathe, incapable of stopping. The angry purple head of my thick shaft staring up at me in as I wank myself silly over David's dead body. "Oh my god."

I'm frantic, desperate to come all over the severed neck. Gripping my cock hard, I twist my fist up and down as I continue to fuck myself. The orgasm building in the soles of my feet and rising up my legs, heavier the moment it reaches my stomach.

As I step to the left, I accidentally kick the severed head and it rolls back and forth on the floor. I freeze. Instantly questioning what I'm actually about to do. I bend down and lift David's head from the floor.

Looking around, I check to make sure nobody may have heard the screaming and come by to take a look.

The last thing I want anyone to see me do, is fuck a severed head.

Pulling the jaw open, I thread my dick into the hole and sit back onto the chair. Dropping my head back I close my eyes as I begin to move it up and down on my strained shaft. The pain of needing to come is unlike anything I've experienced and the quicker I come the quicker I can-

"Fuck that feels good." The words leave my lips as I begin to pump faster and faster. My head dropping back as my mouth opens and my breaths become heavy. The feel of his lopsided tongue as it hangs from his mouth.

The feel of his teeth as they gently drag along the sensitive underside of the veins along my cock. Knowing I ended this man's life because he touched the one thing that belongs to me, gives me an understanding of the situation I never thought of before. I imagine it's Ashleys head that I'm fucking, but that it's still attached to her body and she's alive. Images of her on her knees as I choke her to death, while my dick is thrusting in and out of her throat and mouth, fill me with the most sexually charged emotions.

The pressure building behind my eyes as my eyelids shoot open and, in that moment, as I look down into my lap, I realise what I'm doing.

"WHAT THE FUCK!" I shout. Launching the decapitated head across the room with a thump as it hits the adjacent wall. Chills run up my spine as the realisation of what I've just done hits me. "What the fuck am I doing?"

The bile rises in my throat as the realisation hits me. Fisting my hair, I begin to pace the floor in front of the body before me as the panic settles in my chest and it's then that I look down and notice my dick hasn't gone soft.

"What's wrong with you!? Go down! God damn it!!" I scream at the hardened appendage. "I'm gonna be sick." Is all I manage to get out, before the vomit practically projectiles from my throat.

Nathan

The body of Francesca was found in a shallow grave, two miles outside of Providence in the early hours of this morning. Coincidentally, by someone on a morning run. I'm currently sitting in my office as two officers ask me questions regarding Fran.

Lieutenant Patrick Jones and Lieutenant Angela Mayfield sit across from me. Not only that, but the body of Joseph Chambers was also found this morning. Suspected heart attack over the weekend. Can't say I'm really surprised with the way the man eats. Two people. One found, one fresh.

All in the space of a few hours of each other and honestly, I'm a little shocked. In the back of my mind, I didn't think Fran would ever be found. I don't even think anything other than relief entered my head when I heard she was missing.

The stupid bitch had been blackmailing me for months since our last encounter didn't end so well and I smacked her across the face a little too hard for her liking. Nothing like Ashley though. She's different. She takes everything I give her and more.

Listening to the way she whimpers with every single touch. The way she accepts my praise like she was made for me.

Perfect.

However, since Joseph's untimely death, and as per his request, it seems I've been appointed acting Dean at this moment in time. So here I sit, looking at the two faces of the officers as they sit across from me. One unbelievably beautiful and the other looking at me as though I murdered the girl. Maybe I should have.

"So, how well did you know the victim, Mr Danvers?" Officer Jones repeats for the third time and I'm beginning to wonder how the fuck someone like him got accepted into the police force.

"Like I said the three times you previously asked me… Not very well. She was a student of mine last year until she dropped from my class." I sip my coffee. I knew her inside as well as out. Great pussy, annoying as fuck voice though. "Why?"

"We're just looking at every aspect of her life," Officer Mayfield smiles. "Do you have any idea who might want to hurt her?" Officer Mayfield however, I'm willing to bet my Porshe that her cum voice is delicious. That perfect little pout she's sporting as she looks at me should get me hard but she's just… too old for me.

I've come to realise – after sleeping with Ashley multiple times – that I guess I'm just the guy who likes younger women and maybe I need to come to terms with that. It's the student thing that causes the most bother.

This is my job after all, my life in fact. I'm putting everything on the line yet again for a blonde with blue eyes and the tightest cunt I've ever squeezed into. I really need to stop thinking about Ashley and her little pink pussy before I pitch a tent.

"As I said, I didn't really know her that well and-"

"She was your student though." The male cop who's sporting a huge fucking boil on his nose pipes up again, interrupting me for the second time since they've been here.

"For a year, like I said." I turn my attention back to Officer Mayfield and continue. "When I'm at work my sole purpose is to teach my students. I don't engage on a personal level with them, and I never have."

Yet in the space of a year, I've managed to fuck three.
You're really following that rule there Nathan. Well done.

"Do you have any idea who killed her, Lieutenant Mayfield?" I look between the both of them. Hoping that I might get some kind of insight into what they know or… don't know.

"There hasn't been any evidence found as of yet, but we are still in the initial part of the investigation. Talking to friends, family members people who-"

"May have had a closer relationship with her than many would know." Officer Jones interrupts, yet again. Clearly insinuating something was going on between Fran and I. Accurate.

"Officer Jones, do you have something to say? I feel like I might be under investigation here."

"Should you be?" He counters. The man is feral for an arrest. "Where were you the night of Miss Lopez's murder?"

"Lieutenant." Officer Mayfield scolds.

"That's none of your business," I chuckle dryly. The door to my office opens and Ashley pokes her head through.

Just in time.

"Oh, I'm so sorry professor I didn't know-"

"It's no problem, Miss Porter, please come in. We were just finishing up."

"So, I'll ask again Professor Danvers. Where were you the night of Francesca Lopez's murder"?

"That's-"

"He was with me." I snap my head and stare directly at Ashley. "I'm his TA." She looks between the officers as she walks to stand by the desk.

"There were a few things we needed to go over, and I was lucky enough to spend some time with him at his home while we went through all the paperwork necessary for the upcoming classes."

Leaning back in my chair, I watch as Ashley beguiles both police officers with her perfect smile and believable alibi. She stands there, giving me an out like it means nothing.

Granted, I really didn't have anything to do with the murder of Francesca, yet Ashley stands there in all her glory with a lie that almost makes me question as to whether I really was with her.

"So, as I'm sure you can understand, having a student at a teacher's house out of hours isn't really something the university would be happy with," she looks down at her feet, her hands fidgeting in front of her. "Do you think we could keep this between us please? My stepfather would be furious."

"Of course, Ashley." Officer Mayfield stands up, placing a hand on her shoulder. They smile at each other before she turns to face me. Taking a card from her wallet she reaches over the desk, laying it down in front of me.

"If you think of anything that could help the investigation, please let us know."

"Of course," I nod, resting my chin on my thumb as the other officer stands up, following her to the door. Ashley opens the door for them and smiles.

"Goodbye." The lock clicks into place and she turns around, leaning back against the door with a very mischievous smile creeping up her face. She steps forward, taking a bow and I clap softly, pushing my chair back slightly with my feet.

"Impressive."

"Well, I could hear that asshole pushing your buttons." Lifting a shoulder in indifference, she walks behind the desk, standing between my legs as she runs her fingers through my hair. "I know you had nothing to do with that." I slide my hands up her bare legs.

The tight fitted checkered mini skirt she's wearing does nothing for the imagination, but everything for her figure.

"I figured you might need some help. So, I used my initiative." Moving her hands behind her, she rests her palms on my desk, hoisting herself on top. "To which I figured, you could now use yours."

Spreading her legs wide, showing me the lack of fabric covering her perfect little pussy. My mouth waters as she looks down at me. I pull off her sandals, one by one, dropping them to the floor with a clunk.

"You did so good for me. Without me even having to ask." Sucking in her bottom lip she softly bites down on the plump, pink flesh. "Place both feet on the edge of the desk for me." Complying with what she's told, I watch as her lips glisten with her arousal. Rolling my chair closer to her, she leans back on her elbows, licking her lips in anticipation.

"Eyes on me while I eat you out, love," I breathe, watching her as I flick my tongue out against her clit, her breath hitching the moment I make contact with the throbbing nub.

Closing my eyes, I relish the taste of her against my tongue. "Fucking perfect." Flattening my tongue against my lower lip, I move in closer and glide it from her entrance all the way back up to her clit with a flick. Her head falls back between her shoulder's, and she moans with joy.

Never did I think that I'd have a young woman like this in my office again. I have this perfect nineteen-year-old spread out for me. Mine to do with as I wish. And the only thing she asks me for, is my cock.

"Oh my god." Her breathing becomes erratic as I work my tongue up and down her tight slit. Swirling and sucking in all the right places to drive her insane. Using both my thumbs to spread her pussy lips apart, I poke out my tongue and press it into her entrance. "Fuck," she hums softly. Learning from her past mistakes. Now in clear understanding of when she can be loud and when she needs to be quiet.

"That's my good girl," I mumble against her, the smell of her soaking wet cunt driving me insane. The gentle and fruity scent of her coconut and vanilla body wash encouraging me to stay where I am and pushing all the blood into the correct spot. Pressing a single digit inside her, her hand smacks against her mouth and muffles the scream.

"Jesus fucking Christ, Ashley, you taste so good." I continue to eat her out while unzipping my jeans and removing my rock-hard cock, pumping it in my hands a few times before standing up and leaning over her.

I capture her lips against mine. Forcing her to taste herself. She grasps the back of my neck, groaning into my mouth the moment I begin to push the tip of my cock into her dripping wet hole.

"Remember what I said sweet girl. Quiet... as a mouse." Nodding against my mouth, she circles her legs around my waist. Crossing them together at the ankles. I push forward, giving her every single inch at a torturously slow pace.

"You're so good at taking my cock, love," I groan the moment I begin to thrust in and out.

Every time I pull out, she sucks me right back in with a sound reverberating from her throat that makes me want to obliterate her. This isn't about that this time; this is about her. Every previous time we've had sex in this office, it's been about me getting what I want, what I need, and she has gladly taken it every time.

Fuck, she drives me wild.

"Nathan," she purrs, dropping her head back and I begin to kiss her throat. "I... can I?" Her chest rising and falling as she begins to tighten up around me. Her breathing erratic and the skin on her cheeks a pretty shade of pink

"Can you what, sweet girl? Tell me."

"Please can I come?" She begs softly as my thrusting becomes faster, deeper. Pushing her to the edge of oblivion. I wrap my hand around her waist, pulling her close to me as I rest my other palm on the desk beside hers.

"Eyes on me, my girl," I request in a demanding yet delicate tone. Raising her head, Ashley presses her forehead to mine. Her mouth rounded, breaths flustered and a small sheen of sweat coating her chest.

"Come for me, Ashley." My rough voice deepening to a growl as I impale myself inside her, getting more aggressive with each thrust.

Her chest stills as she stops breathing, reaching the peak of her orgasm. She falls over the edge into oblivion, cupping her mouth and crying out into her palm. I follow her and shoot warm cum deep inside her.

Pulling out of her, I watch as it begins to seep out of her. Dropping to my knees, I suck what I can out of her and hold it in my mouth as I stand.

Having my own cum in my mouth is nothing to me. It's not the worst thing I've ever done. Pressing my thumb to her jaw, I hold it open as I dribble the contents into her mouth. "Swallow," I smile. "Can't have a single part of us wasted." The moment I see her throat bob, I thrust back into her and chase the next high.

ASHLEY

"**Y**ou've barely even been to practice with us." Am I really sitting here listening to this right now? "And when you are here, your mind is elsewhere."

Mia crosses her arms in front of me as I sit on the bench. All the other girls, including Captain Fire Crotch are watching intently, waiting for something to be said. The ginger bitch has the biggest smile on her face right now, and all I want to do is smash her face in with the brass knuckles I carry in my backpack.

The way they're all staring at me, judging me, like I need to be reformed in some weird way, just because I have better things to do than spend my days cheering. Watching me like this is some kind of intervention. The fact that Mia is even talking to me like this isn't surprising.

I thought she was ok at first but the longer she's been a cheerleader, the more she's mimicking that of a vile human being. Her face is blotchy and red, with a look on her face of total distain for my presence here.

I knew it wouldn't take long before she ended up just like the others. I have zero patience for people who act like they're better than others. Still, none of them are on my list and the moment I start murdering people who aren't part of my revenge plot, that's when I become a psychopath myself.

I'm distracted for a second the moment I notice them. Walking by the chain gate in the middle of what seems to be a heated conversation. Jesse's arms flying everywhere with a look of panic on his face. I wonder what's got him so riled up.

Besides the fact that Nathan was fucking Fran last year, I was under the impression they never spoke.

"So?" I lean back nonchalantly, settling back to the conversation at hand. Bracing my elbows on the seat behind me, I look at all the faces staring me down. "I have other things to do."

"Other things," Mia scoffs, looking at her perfectly white trainers as she braces her hands on her hips.

She's pissed and if I were a more caring person, I'd feel really bad. But I don't. I don't care about this stupid little cheer team. I don't even care about the fact that Mia is upset because she's not upset, she's only acting this way because of who she's hanging around with now.

I joined initially so Jesse would notice me and coincidentally, he's a bigger whore than I thought and spotted me quicker than I expected. I don't know if that says more about him, or more about what I look like.

I haven't seen or spoken to my preppy little roommate for over two weeks now and if I'm honest, it's not affected my life in any way. So far, I'm doing exactly what I set out to do and as far as I'm concerned, that's great.

"Yes Mia, other things. I didn't even want to join this shit show." Flicking my hand in a line, addressing all the girls behind her. "This was a you thing."

Forgive me if I have revenge and murder on my mind. I have a list of things I need to achieve before I go and cheerleading, wasn't on the list. This was Maisy's thing. The preppy, happy, go-lucky girl, and I was the dark side of her. The little villain.

The one who took care of everything and everyone who tried to hurt her.

"Maybe if you made an effort to be normal, Ashley, people wouldn't look at you like some kind of fucking freak," Mia snaps, fisting her hands by her sides.

Raising my eyebrows, I tilt my head and smirk. "There it is," I chuckle. "Mia, who said I actually give a shit about any of this?"

"I tried getting you involved in this cheer team. So, you could make some friends." Her tone getting higher as she speaks. Frustration etched into her every word.

"I didn't want you to. I was fine the way I was."

"What? Walking around school like a sad little girl. Dark clothing and an attitude to match. Hating everything and everyone. You don't make any effort with anything other than that stupid TA position, and you act like the world owes you something." Taking a deep breath, she continues. "You're a loser, Ashley, and I tried to make you something more than that. We all gave you an in."

"Wow. Nice, Mia." I clap my hands together. "It took you all of two weeks to become a heinous bitch." Swinging my backpack over my shoulder, I step down from the bench, shoulder checking Mia on the way past.

"No wonder your best friend stop talking to you. I'd kill myself if I had you as a friend." I freeze up. The words bleeding into my skin, washing over me like waves of blame and hatred for myself.

You weren't there, Ashley.

I face Mia, walking the few steps before I'm in her face. Rearing back, her eyes widen in fear as my fist connects with her jaw. She drops to the floor, cupping her mouth and the rest of the girls scramble around her screaming.

What a bunch of pussies. Jesus.

"Don't you ever mention her again," I point at her. "If you do, I'll fucking kill you, Mia." I immediately turn on my heels and expand the distance between us as they scream profanities behind me. As soon as I make it out of the gate, Sarah Chambers and Elena Michaels walk across my path, arm in arm as they laugh and joke with each other.

Jesus, you wouldn't think their friend was just murdered a few days ago. I can't take my eyes off of them as they walk through the iron gates at the front of the building. Checking my watch, I look at the time and realise where they're heading.

Once the both of them are out of the picture, I can move onto the final act. I wonder if there will be a case study on me. The revenge killer from Brown.

I laugh to myself as I follow them out of the school gate and watch as they get into the car and drive off. The best part about being unnoticeable, boring, and uninterested in anything, is that people like them, tend to ignore you. If I'm being totally honest, people like me tend to fall into the background and are forgotten about.

We don't exist in their world, and they're so wrapped up within their own egos, while walking around with main character syndrome, that they don't even think there could be someone else around. That's ok though, they'll see me soon enough. And by then, it'll be far too late.

I think I might be the luckiest person alive right now, because the swimming centre Sarah and Elena train in, just so happens to back onto a park.

Like what re the odds?

It's like someone above, some greater being, is on my side. I'm yet again sitting in the darkness of the tree line, like a fucking vampire lord or a... serial killer. My chest shakes with a silent laugh as I throw some popcorn in my mouth and wait for the show to begin.

I set a trap you see. Something that will cause so much pain, and absolutely no way for them to rid themselves from it. They're always together and I might be hell bent on killing right now, but the fact of the matter is, I'd be incapable of taking two at once.

I'm not Batman after all. So, considering these two cock sucking bitches are joined at the hip, I had to think smart. And boy, did I come up with something so perfect, I wish Maisy was here to see it. I scoured the internet for hours, watching all kinds of videos and asking all kinds of questions on Marine chatrooms, claiming to need this for a book I'm writing.

People can be so fucking stupid when they think they're going to get a mention on the acknowledgments page.

Fucking morons.

The only sound up until this moment is my loud chewing. Twigs snap behind me, but I'm far too invested in this to care and honestly, it can only be one person. Turning my head slightly, I look up to the person standing above me and I'm greeted with those dark eyes again.

Seering into me like a kindred spirit; the way death stares into the eyes of wandering souls on their final journey into the afterlife. If there is one, I truly hope I get to meet Maisy there. Just so I can tell her that she didn't suffer for nothing.

That her life, *and* her death meant something, to someone. To me. I waited long enough to make my move on these fuckers, and they deserve to experience unprecedented pain.

"Following me?" I ask, turning back to watch the entrance of the building. I've been sat here for over three hours and I'm becoming increasingly more bored by the second. Who spends that much time in a fucking swimming pool these days.

"You're not afraid of me, are you?" I don't have to see his face to know he's smiling behind those words. I know he hates this; I know he wishes I would scream and cry or even run. Yet I just sit here. Awaiting the death I've been dreaming about since the moment my mother told me I'd never see my soulmate again.

It still baffles me that I haven't spent a single moment in fear of him. I've been around him twice, and only God knows how many times he has watched me. How much time has he spent near me, just out of arm's reach? I think I gave up on the fear of taking my last breath when I realised, I was truly alone in this world.

Sure, I love my mother, but it doesn't change the fact that I am completely and utterly bored with my life. Maisy gave me all I needed. The light in my perpetually dark life. She was my soul, my heart and every little piece of epithelial tissue that coated my body. Maisy was the very basis of my existence.

"Why would I be, either way, I'm dead," I shrug. "Besides, you're really going to want to watch this one." I smile around the mouthful of popcorn. Tapping the soil, I watch from my peripheral as he sits down beside me. The warmth of his body snatching the cold from me when the nylon of his black jacket rubs against mine, making a weird sound.

"You're the most interesting woman I've ever stalked, I'll give you that." Every word is said through soft laughter. The raspiness of his voice invigorating my every sense. Goosebumps trailing up my skin and I can't tell if it's the night air, or him being so close. I might not be afraid; I am however inquisitive.

"I thought brunettes were your type, anyway." I fist another handful of popcorn and shovel it into my mouth. The crunching of the sweet and salty mixture permeating my tastebuds and releasing that happy endorphin.

"There's a lot I'm doing lately that doesn't match my usual killing pattern," he sighs. Leaning over, a gloved hand snatches some popcorn from the bag as he lifts his black mask up and stuffs it into his mouth. He raises an eyebrow as he looks at me from the corner of his eye, winking at me in the darkness. A playful curve appears on his lips as he lowers the mask back down.

"How old are you, anyway?" He can't be that old, I'm sure.

"Does it matter?" he responds, without so much as a look in my direction.

"You don't look old," I shrug, turning to face the door again.

How long are these bitches going to be?

"Definitely don't fuck like you're old." The laugh I didn't know I had bubbles up from my throat. The sound of his gentle laughter covers me, as the warmth of his breath turns white in the air. It's then that I realise, this is the first time I've had a normal conversation. With a serial killer no doubt.

He stares at me. "That... That wasn't supposed to happen." As though he's looking through every single wall I've built up to every single person in this world. Typical of me to start looking at a serial killer as something more than. I mean, this guy has killed eight women in the past year, and nobody has managed to catch him. Yet here we sit, together, talking like old friends.

Tilting my body to the side I nudge his shoulder to mine. "Considering you cut the hearts out of women you kill; I'd say that's the least of your worries."

He grabs another handful of popcorn, doing the same as before with his mask.

The sound of laughter cuts into the air and I watch as the girls leave the building.

Rubbing my hands together, I wipe away the invisible crumbs and stand. Placing the now empty packet of popcorn into the pocket of my puffer jacket and smile.

"You're going to want to stand for this one." I flick my hand at the side of me, gesturing for him to get up with me.

"What did you do?" His voice deep as he stands, watching the girls open the car and get in. Their shrill laughter making me wince as they close the doors simultaneously not knowing what's coming next.

"Just watch." I bite into my bottom lip and grin like a madman. The ignition on the car starts and for a split second I think I might have fucked everything up. The explosion booms and I flinch, taking a single step as my jaw drops.

The hood of the car twisting in the air like a gymnast as fire engulfs the Range Rover Evoke. The ringing in my ears screams as I focus on the screaming of the two girls scrambling to open the doors. The action has me involuntarily clapping my hands.

"A bomb?" He asks from beside me, taking a step forward into my peripheral.

"Kind of," I chuckle. "I only attached some wire wool to the ignition wires, yanked them through and placed them into the petrol tank. Messed with the electronic locks on the car and well… Kaboom." I mimic the explosion with my hands. "I didn't actually believe it would work though."

This time, I burst into fits of laughter and the sound of his laugh as he joins in, takes me back a little. I watch as the girls begin to smack their hands against the glass. Their muffled screams, and the pop, and crackle of the fire, are the only sounds flying through the air, as the ashy embers dance in the wind.

Their skin peeling away from their palms. The blisters breaking out all over their skin while the red and orange lights dance against our skin and within the reflection of his eyes. His chest rising and falling as he slowly turns to face me. Brushing the hair from my face he smiles.

"Get on your knees." Gloved knuckles slowly trace my cheek. "Now."

This is it; this is the moment he's going to kill me. "Wait not yet I-" Twisting his hand in my hair, I wince at the pain as he pushes me to the ground. He crouches down in front of me, flicking the blade of the knife out, he then traces the tip against my throat, from left to right. I wince as it scrapes against the delicate skin.

"Give me your hand." He breathes, not taking his eyes off of me. I lift my hand slowly, palm up, and he rests the sharp side of the blade against my skin. "Grip it… now." One by one, I wrap each finger around the blade and hold it tightly.

Trying my hardest not to show fear. Because let's face it, yes, I'm killing the people who hurt Maisy, but I still don't want to be cut up either because-

"OUCH!" I shout, as he yanks the blade from my grasp. "What the fuck was that for asshole, that hurt!"

"Take my cock out, sweet girl." He chuckles, as he stands. Gritting my teeth, I fumble with the buckle and zip of his trousers, pulling both the waistband of his boxers and trousers below his ass. Blood trickling from my palm, soaking into the fabric of my sleeve, which I fucking hate because wet fabric is vile. "Now touch me."

His voice softer this time, but still demanding. I wrap my hand around his thick shaft and begin sliding my bloody hand up and down, in a twisting motion as I reach the tip. Coating his cock in blood, my blood.

I bring my mouth forward, pressing my tongue to the tip, catching the mixture of pre-cum and blood that lingers on the head. Without warning, he thrusts the head of his cock past my lips and down the back of my throat and the metallic taste of my blood, invades my senses. I instantly heave at the unexpected intrusion, before he pulls back out, slapping me with his cock. I look up at him then, his eyes even darker than before. More aggressive in nature. My core slick with desire.

"Choke on it, sweet girl, make it nice and wet for me." Without a single moment to think it over, he thrusts back inside and bottoms out. The short, pubic hair at the base of his groin tickling my nose as I desperately try to breathe.

He grips my hair in both hands and begins to fuck my throat, barely pulling out an inch before he's thrusting back in. My chest is heaving and screaming for air. On my knees for a man that who's very hands have caused destruction and death wherever he goes.

The small twigs and hard gravel from the soil below my knees, grind into my skin and I'm riddled with the memories from the last time he had me on my knees. There's something wrong with me.

I could fight him off, bite down and remove the hard appendage from his body. But I don't. I want this. The thrill and possibility that at any moment he could kill me. Grunting he pulls back out and I suck all the air I can into my lungs,

His fingers dig into the back of my skull, and he thrusts back in again. The squelching and intermittent coughing sounds coming from me are encasing us.

"That's my sick and twisted whore. Make me good and wet so I can fuck that tight little asshole of yours." Thrusting back and forth into my mouth like a wild animal.

I look up and notice he's not looking at me anymore, in fact he's looking at the scene in front. Yanking himself from my sore throat, I fall back.

My pussy is throbbing with the need for him to be inside me and I hate it. I hate that he incites this level of desire within me. Then again, am I any better than him for allowing it. He drops to his knees dragging me forward and pushing me onto all fours in front of him while he reaches round to unbutton and unzip my jeans. Positioning himself behind me, he drags them past my ass.

"I'm going to fuck your ass till you bleed all over me, Ashley, and only when you're screaming will I let you come!" I feel him spread my ass cheeks apart and spit on my back hole. Jesus Christ, why the fuck am I so turned on by-

"Holy fuck!" I scream as he slams all the way inside my back hole in one fell swoop. Covering my mouth, he holds back the scream as I cry out into the leather of his glove.

"Fucking scream for me, you dirty little whore," he chuckles from behind me as he begins to move in and out. Not slowly and not fast either, the pace is brutal, and my stretched asshole burns with the foreign feeling of him inside me. "Look at them, Ashley. Look at both of them burning. For you… For us."

His lips reach my ear as he pulls me back against his chest, twisting me into this impossibly weird angle. Thrusting harder and harder, his movements unrelenting. The cold night air cutting into the skin on my bare ass. The sounds of his skin slapping against mine and the realisation that I'm absolutely soaking, drives me crazy.

"Yes! Oh my god, yes!" The muffled words press behind the hand that hasn't left my mouth and I want him to take what's left of my sanity with him when he leaves.

"I knew you'd like this," he growls, biting into my neck. Marking me as his. "Just like I knew your ass would strangle my cock, sweet girl." Just like the first time, he nips the leather between his teeth and yanks his glove off, pressing his fingers between my legs. "You're fucking soaking for me."

"Yes," I cry out when he removes his hand from my mouth. My eyes never leaving the sight ahead of me as sirens ring out in the distance.

"I brought something with me, something I know you'll like." I moan the moment his fingers leave my clit but the feel of him halting his thrusts as he rummages through his backpack, I thrust back a little, needing more of him. He laughs, spanking my left ass cheek.

"You dirty slut. Fuck your ass on my cock. Let me see how fucking bad you want it." His vile words spur me on, press me to bounce up and down on him.

The pain soon turns into incredible pleasure as the fullness of him spreads up my body and into my hairline. The screaming from the car now silent as the flames still crackle in front of us. The moment his hand is back in view, my eyes widen at the item in front of me.

"You're going to take this in your cunt. Nod, if you understand." I nod my head frantically as the excitement of what's about to happen hits me. He slowly presses the dildo inside my core, and I scream out with the pressure of penetration in both of my holes.

"That's my dirty little whore. Now fuck yourself," he growls into my ear, and I can't stop myself from bouncing up and down on him, staring ahead at the crispy remains of the burning bodies ahead.

They're dead, they're finally dead. The girls who made her feel less than the beautiful creature she was. It's funny how they thought, for a single second, that they were going to get away with it. I continue bouncing up and down on both his cock and the dildo that's been forced inside me. Both our breathing completely erratic as I notice the fire truck and ambulance lights in the near distance.

"Yes, yes, yes," I chant. He meets me thrust for thrust, bottoming out and driving me crazy. Black spots popping in my eyes.

"Come for me, sweet girl!" he bellows, and my scream fills the air as the tears fall onto my cheeks.

Diary Entry, Maisy

November 23rd, 2022

I'm writing this because it's the only way I can make it real. After finding him fucking Fran, all I could do was cry. Then I realised if she was going to ruin everything I had with him, I would do the same for her. The moment Jesse turned up at my door, I knew it was a mistake.

I'd never spoken to Jesse on a personal level before and I regretted it the moment I told him what I'd seen. He didn't believe me at first, told me I was lying, that Fran would never do that, and I was just trying to ruin their relationship.

Until I showed him my phone. He became enraged, throwing my phone across the room and smashing it to pieces. I hate myself. I hate that I allowed this to happen to me. But it's the only way that everyone will know the truth. I tried to console him but even that didn't help.

When he eventually looked up at me, there was no trace left of the Jesse that walked into my room. He was something else entirely. He began screaming at me, blaming me for ruining his life and sticking my nose where it didn't belong. Said I was a whore and that if I was going to act like one, he was going to treat me like one.

The moment his fist connected with my face I knew my nose was broken. I remember everything about that night in vivid playback. The moment he pushed my head into the pillow and how my muffled screams bled out into the fabric.

The way his hand felt as he pulled down my shorts and I begged him to stop. I even remember the song that was playing on the radio when he finally pushed inside me.

Huggin & Kissin by Big Black Delta.

The moment I gave up fighting and let him take what he wanted from me. Jesse Richmond raped me in my dorm room at eleven-thirty on November 22nd, 2022. He shattered me into a thousand pieces and took the last piece of me with him.

He made sure I would never be able to come back from this. He told me that because of who I am, nobody would believe me.

Because who could ever love someone like me.

Maisy.

ASHLEY

Jesse Richmond.
 The cocky little shit who thinks he's everything and more. The rapist who hides in plain sight and who seems to have quickly forgotten that his ex-girlfriend is dead. It's like the loss of her has given him extra player points.

The girls in Brown University are fucking feral for this guy and I don't get it. Ok fine, so he has the eyes of an angel, but I know what he's capable of. Jesse Richmond is the devil hiding in a quarterback's meat suit. He walks around this place as though he's God's gift to women and God damn if it doesn't make my fucking ass itch.

When the news broke during first period that Sarah and Elena had burned to death last night in their 'totally expensive car' the school went crazy. Girls running about crying, some collapsing in the hall, while others stood there posting about it on social media.

I've realised a lot since Maisy died, people will only ever come together for one of two things; a funeral, or a wedding. During either of those two things, people desire to be included. To be part of the day, so they can lie and brag about the fact that they were there.

Sickening really. Anyway, I'm in the cafeteria stabbing my fork into the dry ass meatloaf the cook seems to believe is high grade lunch. The racoon I passed on the side of the road last night, looked more appetising than this shit.

"Well, well, well." I roll my eyes, breathing from my nose as I look up at through my eyebrows at none other than Fire Crotch and her best friend, Jesse. "Look who decided to grace the cafeteria with her unwanted presence."

"Give it a rest Ginger, your mother didn't give birth to you just so you could be a raging cunt."

"What!?" She steps forward. "My mother's dead you bitch!"

Leaning back in my seat, I laugh. "Lucky for her she doesn't have to witness it then." She raises her hand and I lean my elbow on the table, pointing my fork to her face. "Choose your actions carefully, Ginger," I snarl. "I wouldn't want to mess up that pretty little face by stabbing you to death for the world to see." Ginger stills on the spot, fear ghosting her face. Jesse comes into view, pressing his hands to the table.

"Listen, you stupid, little bitch," he leans in closer. "Why don't you just kill yourself. Nobody wants you here."

I feign sadness and turn to face him, settling back into the uncomfortable plastic chair. "Really? It's a shame that I truly don't give a fuck." If this is the best he's got for intimidation, then it's a fail. Ten out of ten would not recommend.

"You could've been great here. Beautiful… popular," Jesse breaths, looking me up and down like I'm his next meal. God, he's fucking sickening. Remind me to vomit when I have the energy.

"Careful, Jesse," I huff. "People might think you want to fuck me again." My eyes flick to Ginger as she stands there, arms crossed, with a look of disgust on her face. "I mean, wasn't it a few weeks ago that you had me bent over the bathroom counter in your frat house, balls deep in my tight little pussy?"

"The difference now though," he leans in a little closer, "I wouldn't put my cock anywhere near you, Ashley. You're disgusting," Ginger begins to laugh uncontrollably.

"Watch it, Jesse," I hiss. Giving him fair warning. "Carry on and something will happen that you won't like." He leans even closer to me, the dry skin of his thin white boy lips grazing my ear.

"But just like I raped that girl last year, I'll come for you soon enough."

Bolting up from my seat, I raise my hand in the air, stabbing Jesse through his hand with the fork I had gripped there. His scream rings out through the cafeteria and everyone turns around frantically to see what's happening. Dragging his hand back, the fork still embedded in his skin, he yanks it out.

"Sick motherfucker!" I scream, pulling my fist back and punching him square in the nose. He falls flat on his ass, and I jump on top of him like a rabid fucking dog. "I'll fucking kill you!" I scream, just as I'm dragged off Jesse, and thrown over the table by none other than his stupid fucking brother Marcus.

"What the hell is going on here!?" Looking up from where I'm lying, Nathan and Coach Peterson stand between the three of us. Nathan crouches down to me, taking hold of my arm and helping me up. "You ok?" He whispers and I nod.

"Richmond, what gives you the right to throw her over the table?" Coach Peterson bellows and I try my hardest to hide my smirk. "Are you out of your damn mind kid?"

"Coach, the crazy bitch stabbed Jesse in the hand with her fucking dinner fork!" Nathan's head snaps to me in shock and all I can do is shrug.

"The prick deserved it, telling me how he's going to fucking rape me and shit."

"What the fuck!? That's not true!" Jesse shouts, stepping forward as though he's going to punch me, I don't flinch though, I don't move at all.

"That's a very serious accusation, Miss Porter!" Coach Peterson snaps. I can already see that he's decided to take the side of his star quarterback. Of course, he would. They always fucking do. I snatch my bag and jacket from the chair.

"Come find me when you want to listen to the fucking truth!"

"Ashley, get back here!" Nathan bellows from behind me, following me out into the hallway. Wrapping his hand around my upper arm he drags me down the hall and into the music room. Pressing me against the wall, he cages me in. A hand either side of my head.

"What?" My blood is fucking boiling and I'm about to lose my shit.

"Did he touch you?" He screws his face up in disgust.

"He didn't fucking have to." Leaning down he presses his lips to my mouth, and I feel disgusting. Pushing him back from me, I smack my palm against his chest.

"Don't fucking touch me, Nathan!" Whipping round, I yank open the door and storm out of the music room. "Dickhead," I mumble.

I took the rest of the afternoon off and skipped all my classes. Including Nathan's. My aim here was to seduce Nathan, so I was able to get an alibi from him at every turn. Seems as though the police here are fucking stupid though, because they haven't connected me to a thing as of yet.

I knew from the moment I picked him out of the roster that he would be the perfect candidate to fuck with. Thirty-eight, handsome and at the top of his field for someone his age.

I'd been watching him for months before I followed him to that bar the night before I was enrolled at Brown. I played my part perfectly well. I also knew from watching him that he had a thing for young women. I guess, I just missed Fran and the fact that he was fucking Maisy too.

The dirty bastard loved going to that same bar to meet with younger girls, take them back to the grimy little hotel room and fuck them. I knew exactly what I was getting myself into the moment my friend gave me that fake ID. What I didn't expect was for the sex to be so good, that it engulfed my mind daily.

Sure, I fuck him any chance I can get but that means nothing. I'd trade everything in, if it meant I could have Maisy back. If I could smell that sweet honeysuckle perfume she used to wear. Sex means nothing to me, it never has. Most people think sex is something that can make or break a relationship.

I, however, see it as a means to get what I want, when I want and exactly how I wanted it. And boy did I get everything I wanted. There's no way I'm going to get to Jesse without his fucking brother being there and unfortunately, I don't look like The Rock.

So, I need another way. So, I figured why not trust someone for once. Why not go to someone who could do something about it. Someone who might be able to help me in a way that's a little more legal.

That's why I'm on my way to Nathan's office. The ugly bitch who works at the front desk has finished for the day by the time I make it into the admissions office. The minute I push through the door I freeze. My hand hanging between me and the handle as I listen to the voices inside.

"What did you think that would fucking achieve, Jesse!?" Nathan shouts. "Saying something like that to her. For what? To make you feel big that you got away with it!?"

What the fuck are they arguing for?

"Got away with it?" Jesse responds, laughter in his tone. "Let's not forget you were fucking my girlfriend for the better part of a year… All while fucking that stupid Maisy chick behind her back."

"Yeah, well, at least she *wanted* to fuck me, Jesse. She begged for me to fuck her day in and day out. You… you however raped her on her bedroom floor."

He knew?

"Yeah, and you fucking helped me cover it up!" Something smashes against the door, and I scramble back. "Big fucking deal." I can't move as Jesse begins to laugh. The echo of his voice permeating my eardrums and deafening me. I'm frozen in time and all I can hear are the words they share between them.

My eyes burning with unshed tears as the pain in the back of my throat constricts my airways. My nose burning as I try to stifle the pieces of my broken heart as they begin to crack further and further.

"I raped Maisy, you fucked Fran and sadly enough, I fucking caught you. So, remember… before you decide to do anything, that *you* helped me, Nathan. You!"

The air is sucked out of my lungs as I slap both hands over my mouth to stop myself from making a single sound. I slowly step back as tears roll down my cheeks and pool at the crease where my hands meet them.

"You helped me do it!" Jesse screams again. "You help me hide it!" The words ringing in my ears as they snap me out of my trance.

"Get the fuck out of my office!" Nathan bellows. His voice fills the room, causing me to back up further and further.

"I'll leave. That's fine. Just remember your fucking involvement in that shit!"

Then I run. I run as fast as my legs will take me. The soles of my trainers slapping against the linoleum flooring as I speed through the hallway. My chest heaving and my heart beating a thousand times per minute. I feel sick. There's no way I could've missed that. How did I miss that? There was nothing in her diary that mentioned Nathan by name.

Not a single fucking page. Not like the others.

Holding my arms out I run into the front doors to the school and immediately turn left. Hugging the brick wall as I drop to the floor. I'm hyperventilating. My chest is in agony. Smashing my head back against the brick wall, I scream the tears from my eyes.

That's when it hits me. My mouth fills with moisture. Crouching onto my hands and knees, I retch. Vomit spreading onto the grass below as I cry through it. My sobs the only thing I can hear. The only thing that's choking me. Two black boots move into my eyeline, and I look up from the floor.

Please help me.

Crouching down to eye level he grasps my shoulders, pulling me to stand, wrapping me in a tight embrace. I can't breathe. I can't think… I can't even speak the words. All I can do is feel.

"Tell me what you need, sweet girl."

ASHLEY

I've never asked for help in my life.

Whatever I need to do, I'm quite capable of doing it myself. Nice and easy. Without having to owe anyone anything after. This is the final act. The last night before I reveal everything to everyone. There's no room for mistakes and absolutely no time to lose.

So here I sit, in a dark and musty warehouse with a serial killer roaming somewhere in the darkness. After yesterday's revelation, and the first breakdown I've had since Maisy, I've had time to get my shit together. I asked him for help, and he so willingly gave it to me.

I made a deal with the devil that if he just gave me tonight, if he helped me finish, every single ounce of help he could muster up, that I'll willing get on my knees for him to take my life.

All he did was smile and say; 'I'm at your service sweet girl.' And to his credit, he has been absolute perfection since. What does it matter if I die after all this? Maisy's gone, my mother hasn't bothered to reach out to me since we came here last month, and the police have no fucking idea that I've committed all these heinous acts of violence.

So just like Maisy, I guess nobody cares about me either. The groaning in front of me drags me from my dissociation and I blink a few times to clear the dancing things in my eyes that you get after staring for too long. I cross one leg over the other and watch as Marcus Richmond comes to. Rolling his droopy head to the left, he finally locks eyes with me.

"What… the fuck?" He coughs a few times to clear his throat and I watch as the realisation hits him that he's tied to a chair.

His arms behind his back, his ankles tied separately to each chair leg in front. Rope wrapped around his torso and one around his throat. He's completely naked and looking at his shrunken cock, it's not bad. I'm sitting in the darkest corner of the room, watching him panic and trying to pull free from his restraints.

"It's no good." I call out.

"Who's that!?" he shouts. I push to stand from the chair and make my way out of the darkness and into the glow of the small light that creates a circle around him. Narrowing his eyes to focus on me, his eyebrows shoot up when he realises who has him tied to a chair in the middle of nowhere. "Untie me, you bitch!" I take a few more steps and crouch down in front of him.

"I don't think I will. You see, weirdly enough, I don't have any beef with you. You're just too involved with your adopted brother, and I can't have that," I chuckle, playing with the dirt by my feet. "I decided to do a little stalking with the both of you last night."

"You're fucking sick," he spits, still struggling in the restraints.

"Not as sick as you fucking your brother," I chuckle, standing up and taking a seat on his lap. "Seems like you really love having his cock shoved up your ass, don't you, Marcus." I laugh even harder.

"Fuck you!" He looks away from me.

"In all honesty when I watched from the trees outside your bedroom window last night, I was quite impressed you took the whole thing." I tap his nose as he looks at me, his eyes red with anger, but I can see the fear behind them. "A brothers love huh."

"That's my good boy, take every inch in your ass," I mimic Jesse's voice.

"Yes, daddy, fuck yes," I mimic Marcus.

"Shut the fuck up!" He shouts in my face.

Holding my hands up in front of me I move from his lap and stand in front of him. "Look, I'm not going to tell anyone you prefer the company of your brother more than a woman," I shrug. "It's kind of hot to be honest. I love a good MM romance like most readers."

"Just get to the fucking point bitch!" Still trying to pull himself free from the chair. But there's no use, he won't get free. We tied them too tight.

"Oh, there is no point. I just wanted you to know, that I know… before I kill you." He stills, slowly looking up at me. His face dead. Laughter bursts free from his chest and I watch as he drops his head back. Howling through the warehouse and his voice bounding off every wall available.

"That's funny," Marcus breathes. I look behind me at the dark figure and as I turn back round, I realise the laughter has stopped. Marcus is looking too. "Who else is there?"

I see it then, the fear in his eyes as he looks into the darkness behind me. The realisation that not only was I not joking, but I'm not doing it alone either. Marcus isn't small by any means. The fucker is huge, and it took me and Shadow boy here twenty minutes to drag him into the warehouse, pull him up onto the chair and tie him up.

His muscles bulge from the ropes that bind him to the chair and the panic and fear that's written all over his face is actually making me wet.

"Marcus," I hold my finger to my mouth. "I just want to get this over with and then I can move on with the rest of my night. I have a lot to do and many people to kill and you're taking up a lot of my time."

"You're fucking sick, Ashley."

Looking between his legs, I realise his dick has become hard. No longer the soft little worm flopping around as he swings about in the chair but hard as a rock. Scanning my eyes from his groin and back up to his eyeline, his eyes flick up at me.

"How about this," I tap my chin. "You make me cum, and I will let you go." Marcus huffs out a dry laugh, looking back into the shadows trying to see the man who helped me.

"Look at me." I step into his line of sight. "He's just here to watch. So, what's your answer?" I step forward, straddling him and sitting on the edge of his knees. His swollen and angry looking cock glistening with pre-cum as it stands to attention. "Fuck me and live, or I'll just kill you right now." I unsheathe the knife from my thigh and hold it to his neck. Nipping the skin slightly and he hisses.

"You have fucking problems, Ashley. But fuck it. Why not?" He leans his head in closer to me. "Sit on my fucking cock and ride it." He seethes and I lick both of his plump lips. "You won't last five minutes."

"That's a bet." Standing up, I step forward and position myself over the swollen head of his shaft, lifting my skirt around my hips and pulling my thong to the side I drop down and take the entire length of him all at once. Crying out at the intense pressure as I stretch all the way around him.

"Fuck." He groans, teeth gritted as he looks between us.

"That's my good boy." I lean into him, rolling my hips and feeling every inch of him slide in and out of me. "Fuck Marcus, if I'd have known you were this big, I'd have fucked you after that day on the field." I laugh as I begin bouncing on top of him.

"Jesus fucking Christ, you're tight," he growls, looking into my eyes as he bites down on his bottom lip to stifle his moans. "This is so fucked up. If you wanted to fuck me you didn't have to go to.... shit..." he moans. "To all this trouble to set the.... scene." He drags the last word out.

His mouth forming a perfect O as I begin bouncing harder and faster on top of him, chasing the oncoming orgasm that I'm desperate for. He thinks this is a joke and I can't wait to show him, just how serious I am. I stand up, wrapping my hand around his shaft and slowly pressing it to my back hole.

Sliding down slowly and taking every thick inch. The pronounced veins in his cock providing the most amazing, ribbed feeling. "Oh my god." I moan.

"Fuuuck!" he growls as I begin to ride him slowly. Watching behind him as my own personal serial killer steps into the light. I want him to watch me. "Your ass feels so good, so fucking tight. Fuck!" he cries.

After a few more thrusts. Marcus' balls begin to draw up and I look down at him.

"Come for me!" I scream. The second I feel the first spirt of cum fill my asshole I grin. Whipping the knife in my hand from left to right, I slice his throat.

Blood sprays all over me as he chokes and continues to cum at the same time. I grip his shoulders, using them for leverage as I chase my own high and scream out into the dusty air. Sliding off of his now limp dick. I watch as the light drains from his face. The gurgling of blood as it pours into his throat, and he chokes on it. The entire front of my body is covered in deep crimson but watching him die in front of me has given me the edge I needed to finish this night. But first...

"Don't just stand there, big boy... Eat the cum out of my ass. I don't have time to waste," I say, watching as the man who will eventually kill me tonight, walk around the chair and drop to his knees. Pushing me forward, he rests a hand on each ass cheek and spreads me open. Burying his mouth against my ass as the slurping begins.

I've known where Nathan lived all along. I found that out the moment I chose him to be my alibi. After finding out that he was the one who helped Jesse get away with raping Maisy, I'd already made my decision on how he was going to die.

I sat with my new found serial killer friend and we decided on the plan together. Probably the most fun

I've had in a while and to top the evening off, I allowed him to fuck me again. In a bed this time. In Nathan's bed.

I gotta say, the mask thing… I get the kink now. I'm lying on the king size bed, my head hanging off the side in nothing but the black underwear I decided to wear tonight. Chewing on the strawberry flavoured Twizzler in my mouth, I twist a lock of blonde hair between the fingers of my free hand.

Jesse's unconscious body is laying hog tied on the tacky shag rug in the middle of the floor.

Dried blood clings to the back of his head after Shadow and I jumped him leaving Jim's Bar. He was supposed to meet Marcus tonight, and after Marcus didn't show – because he was still tied to the chair in the warehouse with his throat slashed – Jesse decided it was time to leave.

I knocked him on the back of the head as he tried to get into his Jeep Wrangler, and my little friend stuffed him in the trunk, roping him up nice and tight, and he's been out ever since. After we got him into Nathan's bedroom, I was so infuriated that he had his hands on Maisy, I kicked the shit out of his already unresponsive body.

"Are you going to be much longer? I'm cold." I call out, waiting for him to bring me something from Nathan's wardrobe. The clothes I did have on, are now stuffed in my duffel bag, still covered in Marcus's blood.

"Give me a fucking minute will you!?" He curses.

"It's fine!" I counter. "We have all the fucking time in the world after all." Mumbling the last part so he doesn't hear me.

After hearing Jesse threaten Nathan, I have no doubt that the asshole is desperate to get some revenge. Because who wouldn't after you have probably been blackmailed for the past twelve months. I do, however, have the perfect plan for both of them if Nathan decides to pussy out of murder. But we will see. I don't plan on allowing this night to be over quickly. This will feel like a lifetime to them, both of them experiencing what it's like to be at the mercy of another person.

To be afraid and to be absolutely shattered from the inside out. Then, and only then will I allow them to take their last breath. The man in black comes into view, standing directly in my eyeline. Lifting my head, I roll onto my front and lean up onto my elbows and smile.

"Hey!" My grin even broader now. I kick my legs behind me and swallow the last piece of the Twizzler. Pushing myself onto my knees, I reach out and snatch the oversized black hoodie from his grasp. "Finally, sitting in my underwear was *not* the one."

"Do you know how annoying it is for me that you're not afraid?" Narrowing his eyes, he braces both hands on the bedframe, staring me down.

"How much?" I wiggle my eyebrows.

Shaking his head at me, he continues. "Something really fucked you up, huh?"

I shrug, rubbing my glossy lips together. "Not interested in *this* conversation." Not in the slightest do I want to hash out the trauma I gained from my dead best friend. Tucking a few strands of hair behind each of my ears, the corners of his eyes crease in what

I can only assume is a smile behind the mask. "Will I ever see your face?"

"Soon. You never know. You might be shocked to see your own face staring back."

"I'm not shocked by anything anymore." Leaning in, I kiss the fabric that covers his lips and take a deep breath, taking in his scent. "So, if I forget to say it later, y'know, before you kill me… thank you."

"You're definitely the most fun girl I'll ever have the pleasure of killing, that's for sure." Standing up, he holds his hand out and I slide mine in to it as he pulls me up from the soft mattress. Pulling the black, oversized hoodie back from my grasp, he dresses me. He pulls the hood over my head and pokes the tip of my nose. Shaking my head, I smile. Moving the thick cotton cuff from my wrist, I check my watch and see we are right on time.

"You know what to do," I sigh, releasing a heavy breath. Leaning in, he tentatively kisses my forehead and I sigh into it, then within a flash he's gone.

I walk over to the leather chair that's conveniently placed behind Jesse and sit down. Crossing my legs at the ankle, I rest them on his torso as I stab the Mahogony side table with a huge butchers knife I brought with me. Lifting the Glock from the table, I pull the magazine out, checking it's still loaded, then pull the chamber back to see the bullet resting inside.

The safety is off and I'm ready to go. The downstairs door opens and closes, the footsteps of Nathan's loafers click-clack along the wooden floor. The sound ascends the stairs on his way to the bedroom.

I slowly exhale and plant a smile on my face. Ready for when he enters the room. Ready for him to see me. The door handle twists and pushes open as I rest the gun in my lap, ready for when he opens the bedroom door. The bag he's holding drops to the floor and the press studs on the understand crack against the wood.

"Ashley." He freezes immediately, his eyes looking between me, Jesse, and the gun in my hand.

"Sit." I tip the gun to the left and showing him where I want him. Jesse begins to move underneath my feet, and I smile. "Just in time." Lifting my legs off his chest, his eyes pop open and he begins looking around the room in sheer panic.

Nathan steadily sits down onto the mattress. "Ashley, what's going on?"

"What the fuck is going on?" Jesse questions, his voice cracking from how groggy he still is.

"Oh, shut up asshole." The heel of my foot connects with the back of his head, and he shouts out. "We are all going to play a game." My smile drops as I focus on the both of them.

ASHLEY

Nathan stares from the bed as Jesse continues to struggle in his retrains. I've never seen him look so pathetic. All I want to do is say what they did, out loud. But that would mean, I'd have to leave them for the cops to deal with and the way the justice system runs over here, there's no guarantee they will be held responsible. So that's not happening…

"Ashley, please, you don't-"

"Don't fucking beg her, Nathan!" Jesse shouts from the floor. "She's a stupid fucking bitch and when I get out of these restraints, I'm going to fucking KILL HER!" I roll my eyes. He has no idea what he's up against, and I can't wait till he hears it.

"Anyway," I begin, widening my eyes briefly in sarcasm. "I heard you both, the other day." I speak calmly and collectively. "In your office." I watch as the realisation hits Nathan, and I do everything possible to keep the smile from my face. "It's no shocker though. I knew right from the beginning, Jesse, that you raped Maisy." I turn my attention back to Jesse, the fear in his eyes gives him away. He might act unafraid, but in the words of Tony Montana, *'It's all in the eyes chico.'* "What I didn't know… is that Nathan here helped you cover it up *and* that he was sleeping with her too."

"Ashley-" Nathan begins to speak but I cut him off quicker.

"I don't want to hear your excuses, Nathan, so let's skip that part, ok?"

"You're fucking crazy." Jesse leans up as much as he can and spits at my feet.

"I prefer the term psychotic," I wink, before dropping my expression to stoic.

"So," I jump up from the chair and walk to the middle of the room, "don't get any ideas. I have someone with me and if anything happens to me, he'll kill you both."

"What exactly do you want?" Nathan asks, a quiver lacing his words.

"Nothing," I sniff. "I've also got someone else on standby to contact the police for me, if this doesn't go to plan." I laugh. I don't, but they don't need to know that. "But what I'm going to enjoy is watching you fuck Jesse's throat with that huge cock of yours,"

"What?!" Nathan exclaims.

"Because I want Jesse here, to feel what it's like to have someone do something to you… without your consent." I point the gun in his direction.

"I'm not letting him do that to me!"

Funny how Jesse thinks he has a choice in the matter.

"Oh, but you are. Because I fucking said so."

"Ashley please this is-"

"Nathan!" I cut him off. "This asshole *made* you lie for him. He fucking forced you to keep that secret," I scream at him. Hoping my performance will work on him and he will take my side. See what it's done to him. Trust me. "For the past year, you've had to live with the fact that my best friend killed herself because of him."

"Maisy was… you knew her?" Jesse whispers.

"Oh... Shit, did I forget to... Never mind." I flick my free hand. "Jesse couldn't just let you fuck Fran could he, no, he just had to rape someone and make you part of it." Nathan freezes for a second.

My words are bleeding into his mind as he begins to listen. I've allowed this disgusting human to fuck me while I've been running around killing the people responsible for hurting the love of my life.

And one of them was hiding in plain sight this whole time... It just fills me with absolute disgust.

"Nathan, don't you fucking listen to her! She's nuts!"

Jesse begins pulling at the restraints, but the more he moves the tighter they get. Slowly his face becomes redder. Growling as I stomp over to the knife, I tear it through the rope, slicing his throat free. His ankles and wrists still bound as he takes a heavy breath. I don't want him dead, yet.

"Nathan, look at me," I soften my voice, my eyes mimicking the action. Pretending to be sad. "He made you lie." Trying to hold down the bile in my throat I take a step towards him. "I don't blame you. I blame *him* for what he did. But if you don't do what I tell you to do... I *will* kill you."

"You can't expect me to rape him, Ashley."

"It's not rape if he wants it. Right, Jesse?" I look down at him. "He's been sucking his brother's dick for God knows how long... I have her diary, Nathan. After this, we can blame all of this on him."

I'm not sure if I have the patience to keep talking to him like I don't want to pour petrol over his body and burn him alive after he kept Jesse's secret, but I have to wait. I need Jesse to know what it's like.

To be used and fucked even when you don't want it. Does that make me as bad as him? Probably. Do I give a fucking shit? No.

"Once this is all over, I'll leave, and you can go about your life and enjoy your career."

Never going to happen.

"Nathan, come on!" Jesse shouts as Nathan rises to his feet. "You can't seriously be listening to this shit! Jesus fucking Christ." Panic is settling into the room and the sounds coming from Jesse are glorious.

"Jesse, if you don't shut up, I will kill your little sister. Amber is at the basketball court right now, no?" His head snaps to me, fear riddled eyes pierce into me and I fucking love it.

"Don't you fucking touch her!" Tears begin to build in his eyes.

"Oh, I won't touch her. I'll have my friend who's roaming about this house as we speak, go over to where she is and kidnap her. Then I will have him bring her back here and fuck her in front of you. All while you watch." I clear my throat. The corner of my mouth curving as I continue.

"Then *you* can see her scream and cry and know that there is nothing you can do to help her. While he ruins her little body. Tarnishing any chance of a normal life. BECAUSE THAT'S WHAT YOU DID TO HER!!!" My throat burns with all the anger I've kept locked up in my body. All the pain I've felt day in and day out for the past twelve months. All the rage and hate and disgust and… Shame that I feel every single fucking day.

I wasn't there to save her.

"So, Jesse get on your fucking knees and suck his cock. And if you suck it good enough," I grin. "I might not kill you."

Jesse closes his eyes. "FUCK!!!" his voice gruff. Trying to sound like he isn't petrified, when I can see the fear written all over his pathetic face. "Ashley... Fuck!" He shouts again, struggling to get to his knees. "Look, I'm fucking sorry ok. I didn't... I was angry I-"

"So, you raped her?" I look at Nathan as he stares down at Jesse, shaking his head in disgust. "You were pissed off because I was fucking Fran, so instead of calling me out on my shit, you raped someone who had nothing to do with it." I don't even realise what's happened until Jesse hits the floor and blood spills from his nose. I snap to Nathan, his hand shaking in a tight fist.

"That was unexpected." I nudge the gun in Jesse's direction, my eyes still fixed on Nathan as his chest heaves in and out. "Keep going." This might actually be better than I anticipated. Jesse looks between us, spitting blood from his mouth just before Nathan stands over him, his shirt twisted in his hand.

Dragging his arm back, he makes a tight fist and begins beating the shit out of Jesse. Over and over again, he rains down blow after blow on Jesse's face. The crunch of Jesse's ocular bone as it breaks, has him bellowing out in pain. His skin splits and cracks, blood splattering everywhere.

"You!"

Punch.

"Fucking!"

Punch.

"Asshole!!"
Punch.

There is hardly anything left of Jesse's face as he lays there twitching on the carpet. With him being hit in the same spot continuously, his eye has popped out of the socket. Gargling reverberates from Jesse's throat, and he chokes on his final breath.

"Holy shit!" I burst out laughing. Nathan stumbles back as he falls against the bed. "I think," I take a few steps forward and look down at his lifeless body. "I think you killed him." The moment I turn around, my head snaps to the left and I hit the floor with a crunch.

Swinging his leg back, I watch in slow motion as he kicks me in the stomach. Pain exploding as I cough through the pain.

"You stupid bitch," he breaths. "Get the fuck up." Squeezing my upper arm, he yanks me to stand. "Did you think I was going to let you get away with pulling a gun on me?" The minute I'm up on my feet, he thrusts me forward into the sideboard. The sharp corner of the wood biting into my ribs and I feel a crack.

Fractured rib maybe.

Twisting his hand in the thick cotton of the hoody he drags me from the sideboard and tosses me to the wooden floor. Laughter bursts from my chest as I watch him stalk back over to me. His face a deep crimson filled with deep rage. Lifting me from the floor with his free hand, the back of his hand smacks against my cheek.

"You think this is fucking funny!" he bellows. "Pulling a gun on me!" He smacks me again, harder this time. "I'll kill you and you can join your stupid fucking friend!" Nathan lets go of the hoodie, my back hitting the ground again. Pressing myself up, with what little energy I have left, I smile. Tasting the blood in my mouth.

"I think," I take a deep breath, slowly crawling backwards from him. "That maybe I'm not the only fucking psycho in this equation."

"That little prick had it coming. He had me under his thumb for a year." Shrugging, he crouches down in front of me, a look of disgust forming on his face. "I just needed the right time to get rid of him. Then low and behold you helped me do it."

"You're welcome." I spit blood in his direction, laughing. "Clearly needing a woman to do a man's job. Typical." I wince in pain. Bending down, he picks up the gun, sliding it in the back of his waistband and lurches forward, grabbing for my ankles. Dragging me between his legs, before I have a chance to move, he wraps both hands around my neck. Squeezing.

"Too much fucking mouth on you." The muscles in his jaw tightened with every word that spills from his gritted teeth. Spit splaying from his teeth. Soon, my chest begins to burn with the lack of oxygen flowing through my lungs.

I can feel my face turning red, the veins popping in my forehead. My legs begin to kick underneath his thighs and I claw at the muscular hands encasing my throat. If he kills me now, nobody will ever know what happened. Nobody will be brought to justice.

He will blame me, call me a psycho, and let everyone believe I was crazy. I can't allow that. I allow my eyes to flutter, giving the illusion I'm about to pass out. If he holds on any longer then I will. For the first time, I'm scared. I'm petrified I won't be able to finish what I started.

"Stay with me, love," he whispers close to my ear. Unlatching his hands from my throat. I heave, sucking in the deepest breath I can. "You won't die yet." The sweet feel of air running through me spurs me on.

"You should've killed me," I choke, my voice harsh and my brain groggy. The black spots start to clear from my eyes, and my breathing begins to slowly return to normal. "You won't like what happens when I get hold of you." His head drops back as his chest rumbles with a deep, dark laughter. Clapping his hands together in applause.

"Empty threats kid. I'm the one with the gun now. And when I've fucking shot you, I'll call the police myself and tell them you lost your fucking mind, became obsessed with me, and went on a little killing spree." He stands, looking down at me like he's won.

"Typical." I scoff. Crawling backwards with every word he speaks; I pray that I'm in the right spot to grab what's under the bed.

"What is?" He looks down at me, stalking forward ever so slowly as I crawl back.

"You couldn't come up with anything better than that. It's been used before and it's weak as shit. Fucking idiot."

"You're the fucking idiot if you thought I even gave a single shit about Maisy being raped, or even killing herself. I just wasn't prepared to lose my fucking job!"

Frantically feeling under the bed, my fingers graze the plastic of the taser, and I grip it tight.

"Sure, fucking you was incredible. And it's sad that I won't get to fuck that tight cunt ever again," he shrugs nonchalantly, walking towards me. "It is what it is I guess." The moment he lift's the gun in my direction, I lunge forward, lifting the taser between his legs and pressing the buttons on either side.

The gun sounding off above my head is the indication he missed as it hits the wall behind me. Looking up I watch as my little friend walks in over to me, helping me up from the floor.

"You could've helped me, asshole!" I cough.

"You had it covered," he winks.

"Let's just get the fucker tied up."

Water splashes over Nathan's face and he takes a deep breath. Finally awake after being out for the past hour. That's ok though, it gave me and my little friend time to work. Nathan is now completely naked and tied to the chair.

I stripped him of every item of clothing, before I bound him to one of the kitchen chairs that Shadow brought up to the bedroom. This won't take too long. Mainly because I've already called the police.

By my calculations, I have some time before they get here. Luckily enough the asshole lives further from town in a nice secluded, little house. Which is great for me as the nearest neighbour is twenty minutes away. I plan for this to be over as soon as possible so I can head home. Nathan's eyes open and he frantically looks around the room.

"You're awake. Finally." I smile. Standing between his spread legs.

"You bitch!" He shakes in the seat. Anger emanating from his very being, trying to lunge for me but he's tied up so tight he can't move anything but his neck. Like Marcus, in the warehouse, he's tied very much the same way. "I'll fucking kill you!"

"Hm. I don't think you're in the right position to be making threats." I tap the sharp tip of the knife against my bottom lip. "I've called the police, they're on their way. So, I'm sorry, but I have to make this as quick as I can."

"Alright…. Look. Please just… Fuck! Ashley!" He struggles against the restraints again and again, desperately trying to look for a way to get loose.

"There's no 'look' ok, I'm going to kill you, slowly and you're going to scream for me."

I grab the nail gun from the small table beside him, an item I'm sure he would've noticed before now, but obviously not. "But first, I need to inflict some pain."

"Whoa wait, hold on… lets, shit, please can we talk about this?" His voice softer now, but the faint hint of panic still resides within his tone.

"No," I smile. Dropping to my knees, I press the tip of the nail gun to his feet. "Smile," I grin and press the trigger. His scream fills my ears, and I close my eyes, and take in the sound. Pressing it to the other foot, I do the same thing. Nailing both of his feet to the floor. Looking up from my crouched position, snot covers his face and Christ does it give me the raging ick.

"FUCKKK!!!" He screams as I stand, stepping forward and pressing the nail gun to the tops of his hands. "No, no, no, please Ashley WAIT!" I squeeze the trigger again, on each hand, nailing them both to the wooden arms of the chair.

Not like he has anywhere to go. Blood trickles from each of the entry points where the nails sit pressed into his skin. I smile as I clamber onto his lap. A leg on either side as I straddle him. "When they find you," I lean in, close to his ear, "I want the cops to vomit at the sight of you."

Veering back, I press the tip of the knife against his cheek. "Scream for me, Nathan." His eyes widen as I pierce the long blade through the skin of his cheek, deep to the hilt. He opens his mouth and cries out.

In that moment I begin to slice, back and forth, watching as the blood streams from the wound. Jagged pieces of skin clapping apart. I mimic the action on the other side of his mouth.

Giving him a gaping wound on either side. "There," I grin back at my work. "Now you can smile even in death."

Blood pours from his face and mouth, the bottom parts of the skin on his jaw flapping down, the muscle and fat staring out at me. Running my fingers through the blood on his chest, I lift them to his forehead and write her name there.

"Just so when they find you, they don't forget her name either."

"Y-you'll never…" The words are garbled and messy, just like his face.

"Sorry fucker I can't quite understand you." I cup the side of my ear in sarcasm. "Say that one more time."

Nothing to say now.

Leaning back slightly, I begin to carve her name in his chest. While he sits there screaming, desperate for someone to hear him and help him get lose from the rope that restrains him.

"You're making it worse than you need to." I sigh while continuing to twist and curve the S of my girl's name. "Just relax, Nathan." I start with the Y, "It will all be over soon, I promise."

Her name is beautifully placed over the entirety of his pectoral muscles, and I jump off his lap and stand back, looking at my handywork. Blood covers the entirety of his chest and the tears streaming down his face prove he's finally realised this is it for him.

What he did, compared to the others, is the worst part. He sat there and kept the secret of a rapist and allowed him to get away with breaking her irrevocably all to protect himself. *He* decided to fuck Fran, *he* decided to ruin his own career by having relations with a student… Ok, I know it's hypocritical of me, however I done it for the alibi, I had a reason. His reason was to get his dick wet.

Fucking scumbag.

He flits in and out of consciousness, down to the amount of blood pouring from him. Shadow walks into my eyeline and grasps my shoulder.

"Cops are twenty minutes out. You need to get this over with."

I nod, leaning in and slapping his face. "Wake the fuck up, asshole."

"P-please A-Ashley… I'm s-"

Bending down, I lift the bottle of bleach from beside him and unscrew the cap, emptying the contents over his chest and listen as the high-pitched screams leave his voice box. He cries out like a stuck pig, squealing. Eyes wide and full of fear.

"You'll never hurt anyone again, Nathan!" I shout over him. Leaning forward, I raise my arm, gripping the knife as tight as I can and the realisation of what I'm about to do, smacks him in the face. Bringing my hand down I stab him in the groin, taking his flaccid cock in my free hand, I smile as I slice through the appendage.

Blood spraying, splattering my face and hands, as I slice back and forth in a jagged motion. Skin splitting and snapping back to the groin area as I pull farther and farther back the more the skin is sliced through.

His screams become horse, each one filled with agonising pain as I detach his cock from his body. I lean forward and stuff the severed cock in his mouth.

"Choke on it for me!" I scream, stabbing him in the neck, over and over again. Stabbing him for every second he let Maisy suffer in silence. Piercing his vile skin for all the times he thought of her throughout the year. With every inch that the steel blade permeates his skin, I think of her. When all the strength is gone from my arm and my chest heaving, I drop the knife and it clatters to the floor. Soft hands encase my face and I turn to face him.

"You need to get out of here now. I'll take care of everything else, and I'll come find you when you're ready." He leans in, kissing the tears from my face. "Go to the bathroom, now." All I can do is nod. "I'm so proud of you, Ashley. You did it." Dropping his hands to my shoulders, he turns me and pushes me towards the bedroom door. "There's a change of clothes. Shower and get yourself ready, ok? You'll leave in five."

Diary Entry, Maisy

Ashley,

I write this as my final confession. I had my diary sent to you, mainly because I knew you would know what to do with it. That you would finally see everything. I started writing this after everything got bad for me here. After I slowly pulled myself back from you. I don't want you to cry for me, I had a good life. Up until this point obviously. But anyway, I digress. This isn't an entry to talk about all that. This is a confession, my final confession to you.

I remember the night of my seventeenth birthday like it was yesterday. I remember how I looked at you after you kissed me. After you gave yourself to me in a way nobody ever has before. The way your skin felt beneath mine and how your touch was more gentle than anyone has ever been with me.

I know I told you I was drunk and that I didn't remember any of it, but I did. I remembered it all. The way you tasted against my lips when we kissed. A feeling so strong I thought I was going to die on the spot. The way your coconut and vanilla shower gel smashed through every wall I had ever built for myself.

You were my best friend, and I was scared, scared that something would go wrong and that I'd lose you for good. The look on your face when I told you it could never happen again, is something that is burned into my heart for eternity and I'm so sorry I hurt you. You were fine with it, but I knew you weren't. I know that because, neither was I.

What I'm trying to say is, I should've told you the truth. Told you that my heart belonged to you from the very beginning. I'm sorry that I was too scared to tell you that I loved you, that I let you go through the past two years thinking that you were my mistake.

That you weren't worth loving because you were. I should have told you every single day that you were the love of my life. That you were, and always will be, the best thing that my wasted heart has ever loved.

If I could have a re-do on that day, I would spend every single waking moment telling you that my heart remains marked with your touch. Marked with your sound and most of all, that my body will forever be imprinted with your delicate fingerprints.

I will love you forever,
I will wait for you,
I will always be yours.

Your Maisy.

EPILOGUE

The moment I reach the place where all my happy memories started, I drop to the floor. Wiggling my toes in the sand, watching as it falls between my toes. Looking out into the vast openness of ocean I pull my knees to my chest, hugging them close to me.

My stomach filled with butterflies because this is the beach, I spent most of my life at. With Maisy. I can still hear the laughter frolicking between us as we danced together during sunset. The way we always chose here over every other trip together.

This was *our* spot, and where we always messed around. My chest heaves with unshed tears as I bring my knees closer to my chest and drop my chin onto one knee. Sucking in the air on a wobbly inhale, the realisation that everything I needed to do is finally over hits me. And now… now, I have nothing left.

Gazing out where the sand meets the water, I watch as the tide kisses what's left of the sand as it turns into gravel and tiny stones. The seagulls squawk and dance by the wet sand, waiting to grab whatever they can in their beaks.

The ocean breeze caresses my skin as the salty scent in the air hits my nose. I stopped coming here after she died. Stopped doing anything that reminded me of her, of us. And it was there, that I descended into my own personal hell. Into a world where she didn't exist, and I was still here.

Walking the planes, waiting for the inevitable of when it would be my time to finally see her again. Tears slowly slide from my lower lashes, dropping onto my blue jeans and where the spots fall, the fabric darkens. Nothing was the same without her.

Food was bland and what was once enjoyable, and fun became a constant memory that she was gone. A constant reminder that I was finally alone. That I had nothing left and slowly but surely, my heart grew hard. Cold and detached itself from every other organ in my chest.

This past year has been the worst thing I've ever had to experience. But right now, as I sit here on the beach where we shared our first kiss, I'm finally able to think about something good. Everything I've done up until now was worth every second.

She deserved to have her memory avenged. Thinking about it now, maybe she was far too perfect for this world, for us to both co-exist within it at the same time.

"Breaking news for all those that are listening. Today, police ascended upon the residence of Nathan Danvers. Professor of Criminal Psychology at Brown University..." The news reader relays the information of my recent murder on the radio behind me for everyone to hear. Seems I got out of there just in time. Sniffing, I rub the cuff of my clean hoody over my face, wiping away the tears that haunt my skin.

Thinking back to the night of her seventeenth birthday and how I couldn't stop myself from kissing her natural cherry red lips. I was petrified. I had fallen for Maisy from the moment that I saw her, but back then I didn't know what it meant.

The older I got, the more I realised I was actually in love with her. That she was the most important thing in my life, and I would spend every night dreaming about how she would taste against my lips. I'd spend my days sitting behind her in class, waiting for her to turn around, just to smile at me.

The strawberry smell her hair gave off when she would flick her hair over her shoulders is why I love the taste and smell of the fruit. Tears trace my cheeks and I hate that I'm crying. I hate that memories are all I have left of her. She knew I would avenge her when she left me the diary.

She knew exactly what I would do. It's why she left the last page for me. It's why, when I read her declaration of love, my mind, body, and soul cracked into a million pieces. I don't know when I decided to go on a killing spree, I just knew the moment it came into my mind I had to do it.

"We did it Maisy," I smile to myself. Taking in a deep breath, willing myself to calm down. Tears weren't going to help her now. She was already dead.

"I knew you would." Her voice fills the air and I freeze.

This can't be my mind playing tricks on me.

"Never doubted you for a second."

Maisy?

Slowly, I look up. The sun shining so bright within my eyes, I have to squint. Holding my hand up to my forehead, I create a shield for my eyes so I'm able to see more clearly. When they finally adjust to the light and relax, I'm able to look upon the face of my angel. My Maisy.

"M-Maisy?" I stutter.

There's no way she could be here.

No way I'm looking into her beautiful honey-coloured eyes again. She giggles and it's a sound I never knew I missed until right now. "How are you…" I scramble back. "What is-"

"Come here." She holds her hand out and smiles down at me.

Her smile is just as perfect as the day I first received one. Sliding my hand in hers the radio host continues behind me.

"Police are wheeling out two stretchers as we speak. The bodies of Nathan Danvers and Jesse Richmond were found within the first-floor bedroom of the residence…"

Standing up, I look down at my girl. My Maisy. She looks just as perfect as the last day I saw her. Her long, poker straight, brown hair flows behind her as the wind slices through it like beautiful ribbons. Her beautiful eyes glisten as the light hits the right angle and shows the different shades in her irises.

"B-but I don't understand, you're s-supposed to be…" I stutter, the words caught in my throat as she lifts a single hand, tucking strands of my blonde hair back behind my ear. "What's happening right now?"

"I came to get you, Ash," she smiles. I always had a few inches of height on Maisy. She was perfect and compact, and I wished most days she was small enough for me to stick her in my pocket and carry her everywhere.

"Can't leave you here alone," she shrugs gently. Searching her face, I realise I don't care if this is real or not. She's here and I don't care.

Latching my arms around her waist, I pull her against me. She mirrors me, wrapping her arms tightly around my neck as we stand there for the longest time. Just holding each other. Dipping my face into the crook of her neck, I breathe her in. The smell of flowers, the smell I've missed.

"I've missed you," I mumble against her soft skin.

"I've missed you too."

"Wait a moment, I… I understand that a third body has been found inside the house. It seems that the Danvers residence is now the scene of a murder-suicide according to sources at the scene."

Turning my head and stiffening, I stand straighter, looking at the radio. "A third body? There wasn't anyone else there after-"

"Ashley," she whispers. "Ashley, I need you to listen to me."

"The body of nineteen-year-old, Ashley Jane Porter. Sources claim she was found with her wrists cut in the bathroom, clutching the diary of Maisy Anne Lee. The young woman that committed suicide at Brown University last year."

I stop breathing. My lungs frozen on the exhale as her soft fingertips graze my chin. "Ashley, look at me." Everything is frozen in time as the light shines brighter around the both of us. Drowning everything out. I look down at her and she smiles, sadly this time. "I need you to remember."

"Remember what?" I'm so confused, I don't understand what the fuck is going on. "I'm not… I'm not…"

"Baby." The word stills me, and I focus on her and nothing but her.

"Did he, did he kill me?"

"Ashley, baby, he didn't… there was no *him*…" She holds me closer. "Please remember."

"I... I don't." In an instant the memories come flooding back into my mind as they all cram in one after the other. Forcing their way back into each thought. "When you died, I... Fuck."

She looks up at me, caressing my face. "You had a-"

"Psychological break." I finish for her. I slowly start to piece everything together. Remembering the screaming when my mom told me what happened.

I was such a danger to myself; I tried suicide twice. The feel of the padded walls against my fingers as the memory of me in solitary pushes to the forefront of my mind. The feeling of the drugs in my system, images of me sitting in a circle with other patients. Staring out at the white walls of what was called 'The Breathing Room.'

"You were there for nine months, remember?" Caressing my face and neck. "You finally got out and the first thing you did... Was run away." She speaks slowly, waiting for me to register it all. "You created him to protect yourself from everything. Shadow was your shield from the beginning."

"He h-helped me to s-survive in there." The memories flashing to the forefront my mind. "Helped me get out of my head, helped stop the pain of l-losing..." The words are barely audible.

My throat constricting tighter as I try to speak. "It's like I woke up one morning and he was just... There." I remember now. "He was always with me. In my mind." The day I was finally discharged from the Ohio Mental institution, that's when I started actually seeing him. Realising now that this whole time it was me.

The girls I imagined him murdering, it was just false memories I'd created to shield myself from what I was doing. Attending the university, taking classes, sex with Nathan… it was… all a lie.

None of it existed. None of it was real.

"I killed myself, didn't I?"

Pushing up on her tip toes, she presses her perfect lips to mine in the most searing kiss. "None of that matters. I couldn't let you go alone." She says against my lips. Slowly, I pull back from her.

Sliding my hands around her face, I watch as a single tear cascades down her rosy cheeks.

"It seems as though police have found the diary of Maisy Anne Lee which notes that Joseph Chambers sexually assaulted Miss Lee on countless occasions during her first and only year at Brown and naming Jesse Richmond as her rapist. Ashley Jane Porter's suicide note reveals, in detail, that Nathan Danvers was also a co-conspirator in the cover up of her rape.

The note also explains, in further detail, that Ashley Jane Porter, was the sole conspirator in the murders of Nathan Danvers, Joseph Chambers and Jesse Richmond. The location of Marcus Richmond, Jesse's brother, was also stated within the letter."

"It was all for you." My chin quivering as my own tears fall. "I promised I would get them back for hurting you."

She smiles at me, and the tears begin to fall again. From both of us this time.

"As well as the murders of Francesca Lopez and her two best friends Elena Michaels, and Sarah Chambers. Those of which were also part of what was a bullying campaign against Maisy

Anne Lee. The parents of both Miss Porter and Miss Lee have been notified."

"Will you stay with me?" I pull her close to me. My heart beating so vigorously I'm afraid it will burst in my chest. Her breath sending goosebumps across my skin.

"Always," I whisper.

"Always," she mimics as she kisses my lips.

END.

ABOUT THE AUTHOR

C.J Riggs is a British erotic horror author. She resides in Essex, the home of T.O.W.I.E. She writes erotic horror that is sometimes gruesome, sometimes romantic, deeply graphic, but always with black humour. As a lover of all thing's horror within books and film, she was initially introduced to her first Erotic Horror called Skin, written by Audrey Rush. From the moment she read it, she fell in love with the genre, and hasn't looked back since. When she isn't knee deep in horror or plotting her next book, she's busy watching KDrama, with a glass of wine in her hand.

You can follow C J Riggs on:

TikTok: Riggs1987
Instagram: Sincerelyyours346
Facebook: Riggs Booktok

Printed in Great Britain
by Amazon